# FIRE THROWER

Kartr could see the patroller at the far end of the block. Its pace was steady and unhurried. It paused before each doorway and shot a spy beam from its head into the entrance.

But when it reached the next doorway it hesitated. Kartr tensed. No spy beam flashed.

But its arms were moving—

Kartr hurled himself backward. There was a burst of eye-searing flame, and the entrance was filled with an inferno.

Shakily he crawled on his belly away from the holocaust. Was the robot going to follow him in and complete its mission? . . .

# STAR RANGERS

A Del Rey Book

BALLANTINE BOOKS • NEW YORK

A Del Rey Book
Published by Ballantine Books
Copyright © 1953 by Harcourt Brace Jovanovich, Inc.

ISBN 0-345-32308-4

This edition published by arrangement with Harcourt Brace Jovanovich,
Inc.

Manufactured in the United States of America

First Ballantine Books Edition: August 1985

Cover art by Laurence Schwinger

For Nan Hanlin who also prowls the
stars in fiction, if not in fact.

## *PROLOGUE*

There is an old legend concerning a Roman Emperor, who, to show his power, singled out the Tribune of a loyal legion and commanded that he march his men across Asia to the end of the world. And so a thousand men vanished into the hinterland of the largest continent, to be swallowed up forever. On some unknown battlefield the last handful of survivors must have formed a square which was overwhelmed by a barbarian charge. And their eagle may have stood lonely and tarnished in a horsehide tent for a generation thereafter. But it may be guessed, by those who know of the pride of these men in their corps and tradition, that they did march east as long as one still remained on his feet.

In 8054 A.D. history repeated itself—as it always does. The First Galactic Empire was breaking up. Dictators, Emperors, Consolidators wrested the rulership of their own or kindred solar systems from Central Control. Space pirates raised flags and recruited fleets to gorge on spoil plundered from this wreckage. It was a time in which only the ruthless could flourish.

Here and there a man, or a group of men, tried vainly to dam the flood of disaster and disunion. And, notable among these last-ditch fighters who refused to throw aside their belief in the impartial rule of Central Control were the remnants of the Stellar Patrol, a law enforcement body whose authority had existed unchallenged for almost a thousand years. Perhaps it was because there was no longer any security to be found outside their own ranks that these men clung the closer to what seemed in the new age to be an outworn code of ethics and morals. And their stubborn loyalty to a vanished ideal was both exasperating and pitiful to the new rulers.

Jorcam Dester, the last Control Agent of Deneb, who was nursing certain ambitions of his own, solved in the Roman manner the problem of ridding his sector of the Patrol. He summoned the half dozen officers still commanding navigable ships and ordered them—under the seal of the Control—out into space, to locate (as he said) and re-map forgotten galactic border systems no one had visited in at least four generations. He offered a vague promise to establish new bases from which the Patrol might rise again, invigorated and revived, to fight for the Control ideals. And, faithful to their very ancient trust, they upped-ship on this mission, undermanned, poorly supplied, without real hope, but determined to carry out orders to the last.

One of these ships was the Vegan Scout—*Starfire.*

# 1

## LAST PORT

The Patrol ship, *Starfire*, Vegan registry, came into her last port in the early morning. And she made a bad landing, for two of her eroded tubes blew just as the pilot tried to set her down on her fins. She had bounced then, bounced and buckled, and now she lay on her meteor-scarred side.

Ranger Sergeant Kartr nursed his left wrist in his right hand and licked blood from bitten lips. The port wall of the pilot's cubby had become the floor and the latch of its door dug into one of his shaking knees.

Of his companions, Latimir had not survived the landing. One glance at the crazy twisted angle of the astrogator's black head told Kartr that. And Mirion, the pilot, hung limply in the torn shock webs before the control board. Blood rilled down his cheeks and dripped from his chin. Did dead men continue to bleed? Kartr didn't think so.

He drew a slow, experimental breath of his own and knew relief when it was not followed by a stab of pain. Ribs were still intact then, in spite of the slam which had smashed him into his present position. He grinned mirthlessly as he stretched arms and legs with the same caution. Sometimes it paid to be a tough, uncivilized frontier barbarian.

The lights flickered and went off. It was then that Kartr

almost broke, in spite of his carefully nurtured veteran's calm. He grabbed at the door latch and pulled. Sharp stabs of agony shot from his injured wrist and jerked him back to sanity. He wasn't sealed in, the door *had* moved an inch or so. He could get out.

*Must* get out and find the medico to look at Mirion. The pilot should not be moved until they knew the extent of his injuries—

Then Kartr remembered. The medico wasn't around any more. Hadn't been with them since three—or was it four?—planets back. The ranger shook his aching head and frowned. That loss of memory was almost worse than the pain in his arm. He mustn't lose his grip!

Three planet landings back—that was it! When they had beaten off the Greenies' rush after the ship's nose blaster had gone dead on them, Medico Tork had gone down, a poison dart right through his throat.

Kartr shook his head again and began to work patiently, with one hand, at the door. It seemed a very long time before he was able to force it open far enough for a person to squeeze through. A blue beam suddenly shot up at him through the gap.

"Kartr! Latimir! Mirion!" The roll call followed the light.

Only one man on board carried a blue torch.

"Rolth!" Kartr identified him. Somehow it was encouraging that it should be one of his own squad of specialist-explorers waiting below. "Latimir got it, but Mirion is still living, I think. Can you come up? My wrist seems to be broken—"

He edged back to let the other squirm through. The thin blue spear of light swept across Latimir's body and centered on the pilot. Then the torch tube was thrust into Kartr's good hand as Rolth crawled over to untangle the webbing which held the unconscious man.

10

"How bad are we?" Kartr raised his voice to be heard over the moans now coming from the pilot.

"I do not know. Our ranger quarters came through cc, but the hatch to the drive section is jammed and when I beat on it there was no answer—"

Kartr tried to remember who had been on duty with the drive. They were so ruinously shorthanded that everyone was doing another's job. Even the rangers were pressed into the once jealously guarded Patrol duties. It had been that way ever since the Greenie attack.

"Kaatah—" A call more hiss than word came from the passage.

"Cc." The sergeant responded almost automatically. "Got a real light, Zinga? Rolth's up here, but you know how far his two-for-a-credit shiner goes—"

"Fylh is hunting out one of the big spots," the newcomer answered. "You have trouble?"

"Latimir is dead. Mirion's still breathing—but there's no telling how bad he is hurt. Rolth says that the drive room gang didn't answer at all. You all right?"

"Yes. Fylh and I and Smitt of the crew. We were bumped a little but nothing serious. Hah—"

A yellow-red beam of some brilliance silhouetted the speaker.

"Fylh brings a battle torch—"

Zinga climbed up and went to work with Rolth. They had Mirion free and flat on the plating before Kartr asked his next question.

"How about the Captain?"

Zinga turned his head slowly, almost as if he were unwilling to answer that. His agitation, as usual, was betrayed by the quiver in the pointed neck frill of skin, which would not lie flat on his shoulders when he was worried or excited.

"Smitt has gone to seek him. We do not know—"

"One spot of luck in the whole knock out." That was

Rolth, his voice as usual unemotional. "This is an Arth type planet. Since we aren't going to lift off it again in a hurry we'd better thank the Spirit of Space for that!"

An Arth type planet—one on which the crew of this particular ship could breath without helmets, walk without discomfort of alien gravity, probably eat and drink natural products without fear of sudden death. Kartr eased his wrist across his knee. That *was* pure luck. The *Starfire* might have blown anywhere within the past three months—she had been held together only with wire and hope. But to blow on an Arth type world was better fortune for her survivors than they would have dared pray for after the black disappointments of the past few years, years of too many missions and no refittings.

"It hasn't been burnt off either," he observed almost absently.

"Why should it have been?" inquired Fylh, his voice tinged with almost gay mockery—but mockery which also had a bite in it. "This system is far off our maps—very far removed from all the benefits of our civilization!"

The benefits of Central Control civilization, yes. Kartr blinked as that struck home. His own planet, Ylene, had been burnt off five years ago—during the Two-Sector Rebellion. And yet he sometimes still dreamed of taking the mail rocket back, of wearing his ranger uniform, proud with the Five Sector Bars and the Far Roving Star, of going up into the forest country—to a little village by the north sea. Burnt off—! He had never been able to visualize boiled rock where that village had stood—or the dead cinder which was the present Ylene—a horrible monument to planetary war.

Linga worked on his wrist and put it in a sling. Kartr was able to help himself as they angled Mirion through the door. By the time they had the pilot resting in the lounge the Patrolman, Smitt, came in, towing a figure so masked in head bandages as to be unrecognizable.

"Commander Vibor?" Kartr hazarded. He was on his feet, his shoulders squared, his heels brought smartly together so that the vlis hide of his boots rasped faintly.

The bandaged head swung toward him.

"Ranger Kartr?"

"Yes, sir!"

"Who else—?" The voice began with customary briskness but then it trailed off into a disconcerting silence.

Kartr frowned. The vlis skin gave off another whisper as he shifted his feet.

"Of the Patrol—Latimir is dead, sir. We have Mirion here—hurt. And Smitt is cc. The Rangers Fylh, Rolth, Zinga, and myself are all right. Rolth reports that the drive room hatch is jammed and that no one replied when he pounded on it. We will investigate that now, sir. Also the crew's quarters."

"Yes—yes— Carry on, Ranger."

Smitt jumped just in time to catch and ease that lank, limp body to the floor. Commander Vibor was in no shape to resume command.

Kartr knew again a touch of that panic which had gripped him when the lights had failed. Commander Vibor—the man they had come to believe was a rock of certainty and security in their chaotic world— He sucked in the tainted air of the too old ship and accepted the situation.

"Smitt." He turned first to the Patrol com-techneer, who by all the rigid rules of the service certainly outranked a mere ranger sergeant. "Can you take over with the Commander and Mirion?"

Smitt did have some medico training, he had acted as Tork's assistant once or twice.

"Cc." The shorter man did not even look up as he bent over the moaning pilot. "Go along and check the rest of the wreckage, fly-boy—"

13

Fly-boy, eh? Well, the high and mighty senior service of the Patrol should be glad that the fly-boys were with them during this tour of duty. Rangers were trained to calculate and use the products of any strange world. After a crack up they would certainly be more at home in an alien wilderness than Patrol-crewmen.

Holding his injured arm tightly to his chest Kartr made his way back along the corridor, followed by the begoggled Rolth, his eyes shaded against what was to him the violent fire cast by the ordinary beam torch the sergeant clutched in his good hand. Zinga and Fylh brought up the rear, having armed themselves, as Kartr noted, with a portable flamer to cut through jammed bulkheads.

Even with that it took them a good ten minutes to break the hatch of the drive room. And in spite of the clamor they made during the process there came no answer from within. Kartr steeled himself inwardly and pushed through first. He looked only once at what was caught in the full shaft of his beam and then backed out, sick and shaking. The others, seeing his face, asked no questions.

As he leaned against the edge of the battered door fighting nausea they all heard the pounding from the tail section.

"Who—?"

Fylh answered. "Armory and supplies—that would be Jaksan, Cott, Snyn, Dalgre." He counted them off on the tips of his claw-boned fingers. "They must be—"

"Yes." Kartr was already leading the rescue party toward the sound.

Again they had to apply the white-hot energy of the flamer to buckled metal. And then they must wait until the metal had cooled before three battered and blood-streaked men came crawling through.

Jaksan—yes, Kartr would have wagered a year's pay

credits that the tough, very tough, Patrol arms officer would survive. And Snyn and Dalgre.

Jaksan began to speak even before he got to his feet again.

"How is it?"

"Smitt's cc. The Commander has some head injuries. Mirion's bad. The rest—" Kartr's hands swept out in a gesture from his childhood—one of those strange barbarian exuberances he had been so careful to suppress during his service years.

"The ship—"

"I'm a ranger, no Patrol techneer. Maybe Smitt could tell you better about that. He's the nearest to an expert that we have left."

Jaksan's fingernails rasped in the stubble on his unshaven chin. There was a long rip in his right sleeve, an oozing scratch under it. He stared at the three rangers absently. Already he was probably cutting losses. If the *Starfire* could function again it would be because of his drive and determination.

"The planet?"

"Arth type. Mirion was trying to set down in what looked like open country when the tubes blew. No traces of civilization noted before landing." This information was Kartr's own territory and he answered with confidence.

If the rangers' sleds hadn't been too badly banged up they could break one out soon and begin exploring. There was, of course, the fuel problem. There might be enough in sled tanks for one trip—with a very even chance that the scouting party would walk home. Unless the *Starfire* was definitely done for and they could tap her supply— But that could all be gone into later. At least they could take a look now at their immediate surroundings.

"We'll sortie." Kartr's voice was crisp and assured and asked no permission from Jaksan—or any crewman.

"Smitt is with the Commander and Mirion in the lounge—"

The Patrol officer nodded. This return to routine was correct, right. It seemed to steady them all, Kartr observed, as he found his way into the ranger's own domain. Fylh was there before him, freeing their packs from the general jumble the crash had made of their supplies. Kartr shook his head.

"Not full packs. We won't go more than a quarter mile. And, Rolth," he added over his shoulder to the begoggled Faltharian in the doorway, "you stay here. Arth sun is bad for your eyes. Your turn will come after nightfall."

Rolth nodded and went toward the lounge. Kartr picked up an explorer's belt with one hand but Zinga took it from him.

"This I do. Stand still." The other's scaled digits buckled and snapped the vlis hide band and its dangling accouterments about the sergeant's flat waist. He gave a wriggle to settle the weight in the familiar balances. No need to pick up a disrupter—he couldn't fire it with one hand. The short blaster would have to serve as his sole weapon.

Luckily they had not landed air-lock side down. To burn and burrow their way out was a job none of them would have cared for just then. But they only had to hammer loose the hatch and climb through, Kartr being boosted by his companions. Then they slid down the dull and scored metal to the still smoking ground, ran across that to the clean earth beyond the range of the rocket blast. Once there they halted and wheeled to look back at the ship.

"Bad—" Fylh's chirp put all their dismay into words. "She will not lift from here again."

Well, Kartr was no mech-techneer, but he would indorse that. The wrenched and broken-backed ship before them would certainly never ride the space lanes again,

16

even if they could get her to a refitting dock. And the nearest of those was, Space knew, how many suns away!

"Why should we worry about that?" asked Zinga mildly. "Since we first upped-ship on this voyage we guessed that there would be for us no return—"

Yes, they had feared that, deep in their hearts, in the backs of their minds, with that flutter of terror and loneliness which plucked at a man's nerves as he rode between system and stars. But none of them had before admitted it openly to another. None—unless—

Maybe the humans had not admitted it, but the Bemmys might have. Loneliness had long since become a part of their lives—they were so often the only individuals of their respective species aboard a ship. If Kartr felt alien in Patrol crews because he was not only a specialized ranger but also a barbarian from a frontier system, what must Fylh or Zinga feel—they who could not even claim the kinship of a common species?

Kartr turned away from the broken ship to study the sandy waste studded with rock outcrops. It must be close to midday and the sun beat down heavily upon them. Under this wave of heat Zinga thrived. His frill spread wide—making a fan behind his hairless head, pulsing a darker red with every passing moment, his slender tongue flickered in and out between his yellow lips. But Fylh moved to the protection of the shadow by the rocks.

This was desert land. Kartr's nostrils expanded, taking in and classifying strange scents. No life except—

His head snapped to the left. Life! But Zinga was before him, the big four-toed feet running lightly over sand, the thin webs between the toes keeping the reptilian ranger from sinking into the stuff through which the others slipped and slid. When Kartr joined him the tall Zacathan was squatting beside a rock on which curled a whiplash of scaled body. A narrow head swung up, a tongue flickered in and out.

Kartr stopped and tried mind touch. Yes, this was native life. Alien, of course. A mammal he might have made contact with. But this was reptile. Zinga might not have the same mind touch power that the sergeant possessed but this creature was distantly of his own kind—could he make friends? Kartr fought to catch and interpret those strange impressions which hovered just on the borderline of thought waves he could read. The creature had been alarmed at their coming, but now it was interested in Zinga. It had a high degree of self-confidence, a confidence which argued that it must have a natural weapon of potency.

"It has poison fangs—" Zinga answered that question for him. "And it does not like your scent. I think that you may suggest some natural enemy. But me it does not mind. It cannot tell us much—it is not a thinker—"

The Zacathan touched a horny finger tip to the creature's head. It permitted this liberty warily. And when Zinga rose to his feet its head lifted also, swinging higher above the coils of its body as if to watch him the better.

"It will be of little use to us, and to your kind it may be deadly. I shall send it away." Zinga stared down at the coiled creature. Its head began to sway in a short arc. Then it hissed and was gone, slipping into a crack between the rocks.

"Come here, leaden feet!" Fylh's voice drifted down from the sky.

The Trystian's feather-crested head with its large round eyes, unlidded, looked down from the tallest of the rock peaks. Kartr sighed. That climb might be nothing at all for the birdman with his light bones, but *he* certainly dreaded to try it—with only one hand in working order.

"What do you see?" he asked.

"There are growing things—over there—" The golden arm above his head swung eastward, the large thumb-claw out in added emphasis.

18

Zinga was already scuttling up the side of the sun-baked rock.

"How far?" Kartr demanded.

Fylh squinted and considered. "Perhaps two fals—"

"Space measure, please," Kartr pleaded patiently. In his aching head he simply could not translate the measures of Fylh's home planet into human terms.

Zinga answered. "Maybe a good mile. The growing things are green—"

"Green?" Well, that wasn't too strange. Yellow-green, and blue-green, and dull purple, red, yellow, even sickly white—he had seen all kinds and colors of vegetation since he had put on the comet insignia.

"But this is a different green—" The Zacathan's words floated down slowly, as if Zinga was now puzzled by the evidence before his eyes.

And Kartr knew that he must see too. As a ranger-explorer he had walked the soil of countless planets in myriad systems—nowadays he found it hard to reckon how many. There were some easy to remember, of course, because of their horror or their strange inhabitants. But the rest were only a maze of color and queer life in his mind and he had to refer to old reports and the ship's log to recall facts. The thrill he had once known, when he pushed for the first time through alien vegetation, or tried to catch the mind waves of things he could not see, had long since gone. But now, as he scrabbled for a hand hold and dug the toes of his boots into hollows in the gritty rock, he began to recapture a faint trace of that forgotten emotion.

Claw fingers and scaled digits reached down to hook in his shoulder harness and belt and heave him up to the narrow top of the spur. He flinched from the heat of the stone and shielded his eyes against the glare with his cupped hands.

What Fylh had discovered was easy to see. And that

19

prick of excitement stirred again far inside him. For that ribbon of vegetation *was* green! But the green! It had no yellow tint, and none of the blue cast it would have held on his own vanished Ylene. It was a verdant green such as he had never set eyes upon before—running in a thin line across the desert country as if it followed some source of moisture. He blinked to clear his sight and then, knowing that his natural powers at that range were far inferior to Fylh's, he unhooked his visibility lenses. It was hard work to adjust them with only one hand but at last he was able to turn them on that distant ribbon.

Trees, bushes, leaped at him across the baked rock. He might almost touch one of those leaves, trembling in the passing of some faint breeze. And under that same cluster of leaves he caught a fleck of dancing light. He had been right, that was flowing water.

Slowly he turned, the lenses at his eyes, Zinga's hands closing on his hips to steady him as he moved, following that green streak north. Miles ahead it widened, spread into a vast splotch of the restful color. They must have crashed close to the edge of the desert. And that river could guide them north to life. Fylh stirred beside him and Kartr tipped the lenses skyward, having caught in his mind that far-away shimmer of life force. Wide wings wheeled and dipped. He saw the cruel curve of a hunter's beak and strong talons as the sky creature sailed proudly over them.

"I like this world—" Zinga's hissing speech broke the silence. "And I think for us it will be right. Here are those of my blood—even if far distant—and there, in the sky, is one akin to you, Fylh. Do you not wish sometimes that your ancestors had not shed their wings along the path they trod to wisdom?"

Fylh shrugged. "What of the tails and fighting claws your people dropped behind, my brave Zinga? And Kartr's race once went with fur upon them—maybe tailed

20

too—many animals are. One cannot have everything." But he continued to watch the bird until it was out of even his range of sight.

"We might try getting one of the sleds loose. There ought to be enough sil-con left to take us as far as that patch of green in the north. Where there is grass there should be food—"

Kartr heard a faint snicker from Zinga. "Can it be that our Bemmy-cum-animal lover has turned hunter?"

*Could* he kill—kill to eat? But the supplies were low in the ship—if any had survived the crash. Sooner or later they would have to live off the land. And meat—meat was necessary for life. The sergeant forced himself to think of that in what he hoped was a sensible fashion. But still he was not sure that he could align the sights of a blaster and pull the trigger—for the purpose of meat!

No need to think of that until the time came. He hooked the lenses back on his belt.

"Back to report?" Fylh began to lower himself over the edge of the pinnacle.

"Back to report," agreed Kartr soberly.

# 2

## GREEN HILLS

"—a stream bed with vegetation and indication of better land to the north. Request permission to break out one of the sleds and explore in that direction."

It was disconcerting to report to a blank mask of bandages, surprisingly difficult, Kartr found. He stood at attention, waiting for the Commander's response.

"And the ship?"

Sergeant Kartr might have shrugged, had etiquette permitted. Instead he answered with some caution.

"I'm no techneer, sir. But she looks done for."

There it was—straight enough. Again he wished he could see the expression on the face under that roll upon roll of white plasta-skin. The quiet in the lounge was broken only by the breath, whistling and labored, moving in and out of Mirion's torn lips. The pilot was still unconscious. Kartr's wrist ached viciously and, after the clean air outside, the smog in the ship seemed almost too thick to stomach.

"Permission granted. Return in ten hours—" But that answer sounded mechanical, as if Vibor were now only a recording machine repeating sounds set on the wire long ago. That was the correct official order to be given when the ship planeted and he gave it as he had so many countless times before.

Kartr saluted and detoured around Mirion to the door. He hoped that there was a sled ready to fly. Otherwise, they'd foot it as far as they could.

Zinga hovered outside, his pack on his shoulders, Kartr's dangling from one arm.

"The port sled is free. We've fueled it with cubes from ship's supply—"

They had no right to do that ordinarily. But now it was raw folly not to raid the stores when the *Starfire* would never use them again. Kartr crawled over the battered hatch to the now open berth of the sled. Fylh was already impatiently seated behind the windbreak, testing the controls.

"She'll fly?"

Fylh's head, the crest flat against the skull like some odd, stiff mane of hair, swiveled and his big reddish eyes met the sergeant's. The cynical mockery with which the Trystian met life was clear in his reply.

"We will hope so. There is, of course, a fair chance that within seconds after I set us off we will only be dust drifting through the air. Strap down, dear friends, strap down!"

Kartr folded his long legs under him beside Zinga, and the Zacathan fastened the small shock web across them both. Fylh's claws touched a button. The craft swept sidewise out of the hull of the *Starfire*, slowly, delicately until they were well away from the ship, then it arose swiftly with Fylh's usual disregard for the niceties of speed adjustment. Kartr merely swallowed and endured.

"To the river and then along it, hover twenty feet up—"

Not that Fylh needed any such order. This was the sort of thing they had done before. Kartr edged forward an inch or two to the spy-port on the right. Zinga was already at the similar post on the left.

It seemed only seconds before they were over water,

looking down into the tangled mass of bright green which clothed its banks. Automatically Kartr classified and inventoried. It was not necessary this time to make detailed notes. Fylh had triggered the scanner and it should be recording as they flew. The motion of the sled sent air curving back against their sweating bodies. Kartr's nostrils caught scents—some old, some new. The life below was far down the scale of intelligence—reptile, bird, insect. He thought that this desert country supported little else. But they did have two bits of luck to cling too—that this was an Arth planet and that they had landed so close to the edge of the wasteland.

Zinga scratched his scaled cheek reflectively. He loved the heat, his frill spread to its greatest extent. And Kartr knew that the Zacathan would have much preferred to cross the burning sands on his own feet. He was radiating cheerful interest, almost, the sergeant thought a little resentfully, as if he were one of the sleek, foppish officers of a Control or Sector base being escorted on a carefully supervised sightseeing tour. But then Zinga always enjoyed living in the present, his long-yeared race had plenty of time to taste the best of everything.

The sled rode the air smoothly, purring gently. That last tune-up they had given her had done the trick after all. Even though they had had to work from instructions recorded on a ten-year-old repair manual tape. She had been given the last of the condensers. They had practically no spare parts left now—

"Zinga," Kartr demanded suddenly of his seat mate. "Were you ever in a real Control fitting and repair port?"

"No," replied the Zacathan cheerfully. "And I sometimes think that they are only stories invented for the amusement of the newly hatched. Since I was mustered into the service we have always done the best we could to make our own repairs—with what we could find or steal. Once we had a complete overhaul—it took us almost

24

three months—we had two wrecked ships to strip for other parts. What a wealth of supplies! That was on Karbon, four—no, five space years ago. We still had a head mech-techneer in the crew then and he supervised the job. Fylh—what was his name?"

"Ratan. He was a robot from Deneb II. We lost him the next year in an acid lake on a blue star world. He was very good with engines—being one himself."

"What has been happening to Central Control—to us?" asked Kartr slowly. "Why don't we have proper equipment—supplies—new recruits?"

"Breakdown," replied Fylh crisply. "Maybe Central Control is too big, covers too many worlds, spreads its authority too thin and too far. Or perhaps it is too old so that it loses hold. Look at the sector wars, the pull for power between sector chiefs. Don't you think that Central Control would stop that—if it could?"

"But the Patrol—"

Fylh trilled laughter. "Ah, yes, the Patrol. We are the stubborn survivals, the wrongheaded ones. We maintain that we, the Stellar Patrol, crewmen and rangers, still keep the peace and uphold galactic law. We fly here and there in ships which fall to pieces under us because there are no longer those with the knowledge and skill to repair them properly. We fight pirates and search forgotten skies—for what, I wonder? We obey commands given to us over the signature of the two Cs. We are fast becoming an anachronism, antiques still alive but better dead. And one by one we vanish from space. We should all be rounded up and set in some museum for the planet-bound to gawk at, objects with no reasonable function—"

"What will happen to Central Control?" Kartr wondered and set his teeth as a lurch of the sled stabbed his arm against Zinga's tough ribs and jarred his wrist.

"The galactic empire—this galactic empire," pronounced the Zacathan with a grin which told of his total disinterest in the matter, "is falling apart. Within five years we've lost touch with as many sectors, haven't we? C.C. is just a name now as far as its power runs. In another generation it may not even be remembered. We've had a long run—about three thousand years—and the seams are beginning to gap. Sector wars now—the result—chaos. We'll slip back fast—probably far back maybe even into planet-tied barbarianism with space flight forgotten. Then we'll start all over again—"

"Maybe," was Fylh's pessimistic reply. "But you and I, dear friend, will not be around to witness that new dawn—"

Zinga nodded agreement. "Not that our absence will matter. We have found us a world to make the best of right here and now. How far off civilized maps are we?" he asked the sergeant.

They had flashed maps on the viewing screen in the ship, maps noted on tapes so old that the dates on them seemed wildly preposterous, maps of suns and stars no voyager had visited in two, three, five generations, where Control had had no contact for half a thousand years. Kartr had studied those maps for weeks. And on none of them had he seen this system. They were too far out—too near the frontier of the galaxy. The map tape which had carried the record of this world—provided there had ever been one at all—must have rusted away past using, forgotten in some pigeonhole of Control archives generations ago.

"Completely." He took a sort of sour pleasure in that answer.

"Completely off and completely out," Zinga commented brightly. "Clear start for all of us. Fylh—this river— it's getting a bit bigger, isn't it?"

The expanse of water below them was widening out. For some time now they had been coasting above greenery—first over shrubs and patches of short vegetation, and then clumps of quite fair-sized trees which gathered and bunched into woodland. Animal life there—Kartr's mind snapped alert to the job on hand as the sled rose, climbing to follow the line of rise in the land beneath them.

There were strong scents carried now by the wind they breasted, good scents—earth and growing things—the tang of water. They still hovered over the stream bed and, below, the current was stronger, beating around and over rocks. Then the river curved around a point thick with trees and before them, perhaps half a mile away, was a falls, a spray veil splashing over the rocky lip of a plateau.

Fylh's claws played over the controls. The sled lost speed and altitude. He maneuvered it toward a scrap of sand which ran in a tongue from the rock and tree-lined shore. They dropped lightly, a perfect landing. Zinga leaned forward and clapped him on the shoulder.

"Consider yourself commended, Ranger. A beautiful landing—simply beautiful—" His voice cracked as he tried without much success to reach the high note which might be sounded by a gushing female tourist.

Kartr scrambled awkwardly out of the seat and stood, feet braced a little apart in the sand. The water purled and rippled toward him over green covered rocks. He was aware of small life flickers, water creatures about their business below its surface. He dropped to his knees and thrust his hand into the cool wet. It lapped about his wrist, moistened the edge of his tunic sleeve. And it was chill enough and clear enough to offer temptation he could not resist.

"Going for a splash?" asked Zinga. "I am."

Kartr fumbled for the fastenings of his belt and slipped his arm carefully out of its sling. Fylh sat crosslegged in the sand and watched them both, disapproval plain on his thin delicate face as they pulled off harness and uniforms.

27

Fylh had never willingly entered water and he never would.

The sergeant could not stifle an exclamation of pleasure as the water closed about him, rising from ankle to knee, to waist, as he waded out, feeling cautiously with exploring toes. Zinga kicked up waves, pushing on boldly until his feet were off bottom and he tried his strength against the deeper currents of midstream. Kartr longed for two good hands and to be able to join the Zacathan. The best he could do was duck and let the drops roll down him, washing away the mustiness of the ship, the taint of the too long voyage.

"If you are now finished with this newly hatched nonsense"—that was Fylh—"may I remind you that we are supposed to be doing a job?"

Kartr was almost tempted to deny that. He wanted to stay where he was. But the bonds of discipline brought him back to the sand spit where, with the Trystian's help, he pulled on the clothes he had taken a dislike to. Zinga had swum upstream and Kartr looked up just in time to see the yellow-gray body of the Zacathan leap through the mist below the falls. He sent a thought summons flying.

But then there was a flash of brilliant color, as a bird soared overhead, to distract him. Fylh stood with hands outstretched, a clear whistle swelling out of his throat. The bird changed course and wheeled about the two of them. Then it fluttered down to perch on the Trystian's great thumb claw, answering his trill with liquid notes of its own. Its blue feathers had an almost metallic sheen. For a long time it answered Fylh, and then it took wing again—out over the water. The Trystian's crest was raised proud and high. Kartr drew a full deep breath.

"That one is beautiful!" He paid tribute.

Fylh nodded, but there was a hint of sadness about his thin lips as he answered, "It did not really understand me."

Zinga dripped out of the water, hissing to himself as if he were about to go into battle. He transferred some object he had been holding in one hand to his mouth, chewed with an expression of rapture, and swallowed.

"The water creatures are excellent," he observed. "Best I've tasted since Vassor City when we had that broiled Katyer dinner! Pity they're so small."

"I only hope that your immunity shots are still working," Kartr returned scathingly. "If you—"

"Go all purple and die it will only be my own fault?" The Zacathan finished for him. "I agree. But fresh food is sometimes worth dying for. Formula 1A60 is *not* my idea of a proper meal. Well, and now where do we wend our way?"

Kartr studied the plateau from which the river fell. The thick green above looked promising. They dared not venture too far into the unknown with such a small fuel supply and the return journey to plan for. Maybe a flight to the top of that cliff would provide them with a vantage point from which to examine the country beyond. He suggested that.

"Up it is." Fylh got back in the sled. "But not more than a half mile—unless you are longing to walk back!"

This time Kartr felt the slight sluggishness of their break away, he strained forward in his seat as if by will power alone he could raise the sled out of the sand and up to the crest of the rock barrier. He knew that Fylh would be able to nurse the last gasp of energy from the machine, but he had no longing to foot it back to the *Starfire*.

At the top of the cliff there seemed to be no landing place for them. The trees grew close to the stream edge, thick enough to make a solid carpet of green. But a quarter of a mile from the falls they came upon an island—it was really a miniature mesa, smoothed off almost level—around which the stream cut some twenty feet below.

Fylh set the sled down with not more than four feet on either side separating them from the edge. The stone was hot, sun baked, and Kartr stood up in the sled, unslinging visibility lenses.

On either side of the river the trees and brush grew in an almost impassable wall. But northward he sighted hills, green and rolling, and the river crossed a plain. He was restoring the lenses to their holder when he sensed alien life.

Down at the edge of the stream a brown furred animal had emerged from the woods. It squatted by the water to lap and then dabbled its front paws in the current. There was a flicker of silver spinning in the air and the jaws of the beast snapped on the water creature it had flipped out of the river.

"Splendid!" Zinga paid tribute to the feat. "I couldn't have done any better myself! Not a wasted motion—"

Delicately Kartr probed the mind behind that furry skull. There was intelligence of a sort and he thought that he might appeal to it if he wished. But the animal did not know man or anything like man. Was this planet a wilderness with no superior life form?

He asked that aloud and Fylh answered him.

"Did that bump you received when we landed entirely addle your thinking process? A slice of wilderness may be found on many planets. And because this creature below does not know of any superior to itself does not certify that such do not exist elsewhere—"

Zinga had propped his head on his two hands and was staring out toward the distant plain and hills.

"Green hills," he muttered. "Green hills and water full of very excellent food. The Spirit of Space is smiling on us this once. Do you wish to ask questions of our fishing friend below?"

"No. And it is not alone. Something grazes behind that

30

clump of pointed trees and there are other lives. They fear each other—they live by claw and fang—"

"Primitive," catalogued Fylh, and then conceded generously, "Perhaps you are right, Kartr. Perhaps there is no human or Bemmy overlord in this world."

"I trust not," Zinga raised both his first and second eyelids to their fullest extent. "I long to pit my wits—daring adventurer style—against some fiendish, intelligent monster—"

Kartr grinned. For some reason he had always found the reptile-ancestored brain of the Zacathan more closely akin to his own thinking processes than he ever did Fylh's cool detachment. Zinga entered into life with zest, while the Trystian was, in spite of physical participation, always the onlooker.

"Maybe we can locate some settlement of your fiendish monsters among those hills," he suggested. "What about it, Fylh, dare we try to reach them?"

"No." Fylh was measuring with a claw tip the gage on the control panel. "We've enough to get us back to the ship from here and that is all."

"If we all hold our breath and push," murmured the Zacathan. "All right. And if we have to set down, we'll walk. There is nothing better than to feel good hot sand ooze up between one's toes—" He sighed languorously.

The sled arose, startling the brown-coated fisherman. It sat on its haunches, one dripping paw raised, to watch them go. Kartr caught its mild astonishment—but it had no fear of them. It had few enemies and did not expect those to fly through the air. As they swung around Kartr tried an experiment and sent a darting flash of good will into that primitive brain. He looked back. The animal had risen to its hind legs and stood, man fashion, its front paws dangling loosely, staring after the sled.

They passed over the falls so low that the spray beaded their skins. Kartr caught his lower lip between his teeth and bit down on it. Was that only Fylh's flying or did power failure drive them down? He had no desire to ask that question openly.

"To follow the river back," Zinga pointed out, "is to take the long way round. If we cut across country from that peak we ought to hit the ship—"

Kartr saw and nodded. "How about it, Fylh? Stick to the water or not?"

The Trystian hunched his shoulders in his equivalent of a shrug. "Quicker, yes." And he pointed the sled's bow to the right.

They left the stream thread. A carpet of trees lay beneath them and then a scrubby clearing in which a group of five red-brown animals grazed. One tossed its head skyward and Kartr saw the sun glint on long cruel horns.

"I wonder," mused Zinga, "if they ever do any disputing with our river-bank friend. He had some pretty formidable claws—and those horns are not just for adornment. Or maybe they have some kind of treaty of nonaggression—"

"Then," observed Fylh, "they would be locked in deadly combat most of the time!"

"You know"—Zinga stared at the back of Fylh's crested head fondly—"you're a very useful Bemmy, my friend. With you along we never have to wear ourselves out expecting the worst—you have it all figured out for us. What would we ever do without your dark, dark eyes fixed upon the future?"

The trees and shrubs below were growing fewer. Rock and sections of baked, creviced earth and the queer, twisted plants which seemed native to the desert appeared in larger and larger patches.

"Wait!" Kartr's hand shot out to touch Fylh's arm. "To the right—there!"

The sled obediently swooped and came down on a

patch of level earth. Kartr scrambled out, brushed through the fringe of stunted bush to come out upon the edge of what he had sighted from the air. The other two joined him.

Zinga dropped upon one knee and touched the white section almost gingerly. "Not natural," he gave his verdict.

Sand and earth had drifted and buried it. Only here had some freak of the scouring wind cleared that patch to betray it. Pavement—an artificial pavement!

Zinga went to the right, Fylh left, for perhaps forty feet. They squatted and, using their belt knives, dug into the soil. Within seconds each had uncovered a hard surface.

"A road!" Kartr kicked more sand away. "Surface transportation here at one time then. How long ago do you guess?"

Fylh shifted the loosened soil through his claws. "Here is heat and dryness, and, I think, not too many storms. Also the vegetation does spread as it would in jungle country. It may be ten years—ten hundred or—"

"Ten thousand!" Kartr ended for him. But the spark of excitement within him was being fanned into more vigorous life. So there *had* been superior life here! Man—or something—had built a road on which to travel. And roads usually led to—

The sergeant turned to Fylh. "Do you think we could pry enough fuel out of the main drive to bring the sled back here with the tailer mounted?"

Fylh considered. "We might—if we didn't need fuel for anything else."

Kartr's excitement faded. They would need it for other work. The Commander and Mirion would have to be transported on it when they left the ship—supplies carried—all that they would require to set up a camp in the more hospitable hill country. He kicked regretfully at the patch of pavement. Once it would have been his duty as well as his pleasure to follow that thin clue to its source. Now it was his duty to forget it. He walked heavily back to the sled and none of them spoke as they were again airborne.

# 3

## MUTINY

They circled the crumpled length of the *Starfire* and saw a figure waving from a point near her nose. When they landed the sled Jaksan was waiting.

"Well?" he demanded harshly, almost before the sand had fallen away from the keel of the sled.

"There's good, open, well-watered land to the north," Kartr reported. "Animal life in a wilderness—"

"Eatable water creatures!" Zinga broke in, licking his lips at the memory.

"Any indications of civilization?"

"An old road, buried—nothing else. The animals know no superior life form. We had the recorder on—I can run the wire through for the Commander—"

"If he wants it—"

"What do you mean!" The tone in Jaksan's voice brought Kartr up short, the reel of spy wire clutched in his good hand.

"Commander Vibor," Jaksan's answer came cold and hard, "believes it our duty to remain with the ship—"

"But why?" asked the sergeant in honest bewilderment.

Nothing was ever going to raise the *Starfire* again. It was folly not to realize that at once and make plans on that basis. Kartr did now what he seldom dared to attempt, tried to read the surface mind of the arms officer.

There was worry there, worry and something else—a surprising, puzzling resentment when Jaksan thought of him, Kartr, or of any of the rangers. Why? Did it stem back to the fact that the ranger sergeant was not a child of the Service, had not been reared of a Patrol family in the tight grip of tradition and duty, as had the other human members of the crew? Was it because he was termed a Bemmy lover and alien? He accepted that resentment as a fact, pigeonholed the memory of it to recall when he had to work with Jaksan in the future.

"Why?" The arms officer repeated Kartr's question. "A commander has responsibilities—even a ranger should realize that. Responsibilities—"

"Which doom him to starve to death in a broken ship?" cut in Zinga. "Come now, Jaksan. Commander Vibor is an intelligent life form—"

Kartr's fingers moved in the old warning signal. The Zacathan caught it and was silent while the sergeant cut in quickly on the heels of the other's last word.

"He will undoubtedly wish to see the record tape before making any plans anyway."

"The Commander is blind!"

Kartr stopped short. "You are sure?"

"Smitt is. Tork might have been able to help him. We don't have the skill—the wounds go beyond the help of the medic-first-aid."

"Well, I'll report." Kartr started toward the ship, feeling as if he carried several pounds of star-lead in the sole of each boot and some vast and undefinable burden had settled down upon his shoulders.

Why, he asked himself dispiritedly as he climbed through the lock of the port, did he have this depression? Certainly leadership now in no way fell upon him. Both Jaksan and Smitt outranked a sergeant—as a warrant officer of rangers he was just barely within the borderline of the Service as it was. But even knowing that did nothing to free him from this unease.

"Kartr reporting, sir!" He came to attention before the masked man propped up against two bedrolls in the lounge.

"Your report—" The request was mechanical. Kartr began to wonder if the other really heard him, or, hearing, understood a word he said.

"We have crashed near the edge of a desert. By sled the scouting party traveled north along a river to a well-watered, forested tract. Because of the limited supply of fuel our cruising range was curtailed. But there is a section to the north which looks promising as a base for a camp—"

"Life indications?"

"Many animals of different types and breeds—on a low scale of intelligence. Only trace of civilization is a portion of roadway so covered as to argue long disuse. Animals have no memory of contact with superior life forms."

"Dismissed."

But Kartr did not go. "Pardon, sir, but have I your permission to break out what is left of the main drive energy supply to use when we arrange for transportation—"

"The ship's supply? Are you completely mad? Certainly not! Report to Jaksan for repair party duty—"

Repair party? Did Vibor honestly believe that there was the slightest chance of repairing the *Starfire?* Surely— The ranger hesitated at the door of the lounge and half turned to go back. But, guessing the uselessness of any further appeal made to Vibor, he went on to the rangers' quarters where he found the others gathered. A smaller figure just within the doorway turned out to be Smitt, who got up to face Kartr as he came in.

"Any luck, Kartr?"

"He told me to report for repair party duty. Great Winds of Space, what does he mean?"

"You may not believe it," answered the com-techneer, "but he means just what he says. We are supposed to be repairing this hulk for a take-off—"

"But can't he see—?" began Kartr and then bit his lip, remembering. That was just it—the Commander could not see the present condition of the wrecked ship. But that was no excuse for Jaksan or Smitt not making it plain to him—

As if he was able to pick that thought out of the air the com-techneer answered:

"He won't listen to us. I was ordered to my quarters when I tried to tell him. And Jaksan's only agreed with every order he's issued!"

"But why did he do that? Jaksan's no fool, he knows that we aren't going to lift again. The *Starfire's* done for."

Smitt leaned back against the wall. He was a small man, thin and tough and almost black with space tan. And now he appeared to share a portion of Fylh's almost malicious detachment. The only things he had ever really loved were his communicators. Kartr had seen him once furtively stroking the smooth plastic of their sides with a loving hand. Because of the old division of the ship's personnel—Patrol crew and rangers—Kartr did not know him very well.

"You can easily accept the idea that we're through," the com-techneer was saying now. "You've never been tied to this hunk of metal the way we are. Your duty is on planets—not in space. The *Starfire* is a part of Vibor—he can't just walk into the wide blue now and forget all about her— Neither can Jaksan."

"All right. I can believe that the ship might mean more to you, her regular crew, than she does to us," agreed Kartr almost wearily. "But she's a dead ship now and nothing any of us or all of us can do will make her ready to lift again. We'd best leave her—try to establish a base somewhere near food and water—"

"Cut clean from the past and begin again? Maybe. I can agree with you—intellectually. Only in suggesting that you'll come up against emotions, too, my young friends. And you'll find that another matter altogether!"

"And why," asked Kartr slowly, "is it up to *me* to deal with anything?"

"Process of elimination elects you. If we're grounded past hope of escape, who is the best able to understand our problems—someone who has spent his life in space almost since childhood—or a ranger? What *are* you going to do?"

But Kartr refused to answer that. The longer Smitt needled him in that fashion the more uneasy he became. He had never been treated with such frankness by a crew officer.

"The Commander will decide," he began.

Then Smitt laughed, a short harsh sound which lacked any thread of mirth. "So you're afraid to face up to it, fly-boy? I thought you rangers could never be rattled— that the fearless, untamed explorers would—"

Kartr's good hand closed on the tunic folds just below Smitt's throat.

"What kind of trouble are you trying to start, Smitt?" he asked, omitting the respect due an officer.

But the com-techneer made no move to strike away the sergeant's hand or twist free from the hold. Instead his eyes lifted to meet Kartr's steadily, soberly. Kartr's fingers loosened and his hand dropped. Smitt believed in what he was trying to say, believed in it very much even though he had been jeering. Smitt had come to him for help. Now for the first time Kartr was glad he possessed that queer gift of his—to sense the emotions of his fellows.

"Let's have it," he said and sat down on a bedroll. He was aware that the tension which had held them all for a second or two was relaxing. And he knew that the rangers would follow his lead—they would wait for his decision.

"Vibor is no longer with us—he's—he's cracked." Smitt fumbled for words. And Kartr read in him a rising fear and desolation.

"Is it because of his loss of sight? If that is so, the condition may be only temporary. When he becomes resigned to that—"

"No. He has been heading for a breakdown for a long time. The responsibility of command under present conditions—that fight with the Greenies—he was good friends with Tork, remember? The ship falling to pieces bit by bit and no chance for repairs— It's added up to drive him under. Now he's just refusing to accept a present he doesn't dare believe in. He's retired into a world of his own where things go right instead of wrong. And he wants us in there with him."

Kartr nodded. There was the ring of truth in every word Smitt said. Of course, he himself had never had much personal contact with Vibor. The rangers were not admitted to the inner circle of the Patrol—they were only tolerated. He was not a graduate of a sector academy, or even a product of the ranks. His father had not been Patrol before him. So he had always been aloof from the crew. The discipline of the Service, always strict, had been tightening more and more into a rigid caste system, even during the few years he had worn the Comet—perhaps because the Service itself had been cut off from the regular life of the average citizens. But Kartr could at this moment understand the odd incidents of the past months, certain inconsistencies in Vibor's orders—one or two remarks he had overheard.

"You think that there is no chance of his recovering?"

"No. The crash pushed him over the edge. The orders he's given during the past hour or so— I tell you—he's finished!"

"All right." Rolth's low voice cut through the thick air.

"Then what do we do—or rather, what do *you* want us to do, Smitt?"

The com-techneer's hands spread out in a gesture of hopelessness.

"I don't really know. Only we're down—permanently—on an unknown world. Exploration—that's your department. And somebody's got to take the lead in getting us out of here. Jaksan—well, he might follow the Commander even if Vibor says blast us and the ship. They went through the battle of the Five Suns together and Jaksan—" His voice trailed off.

"What about Mirion?"

"He isn't conscious. I don't think he's going to pull through. We can't even tell how badly he's injured. He can be counted out."

Counted out of what, wondered Kartr, and his green eyes narrowed. Smitt was hinting now of some kind of conflict to come.

"Dalgre and Snyn?" asked Zinga.

"They're both Jaksan's squadmen. Who knows how they'll stand if he starts giving orders?" returned the com-techneer.

"There is one thing I find puzzling." Fylh broke in for the first time. "Why do you come to us, Smitt? We're not crew—"

There was the question which had been in all their minds—at last brought into the open. Kartr waited for the answer to it.

"Why—well, because I think that you're the best equipped for the future. It's your job. I'm dead weight now anyway—the crash did for the coms. The crew's dead weight without a ship to raise. So, all right—we should be ready to learn what it takes to keep on living—"

"A recruit, is it?" Zinga's chuckle was more hiss. "But

41

a very green one. Well, Kartr, do you sign him?" The Zacathan's grotesque head turned to the sergeant.

"He's speaking the truth," Kartr returned very soberly. "I call council!" He gave the order which alerted them all. "Rolth?"

That white-skinned face, more than half masked by the dark goggles, was hard to read.

"The land is good?"

"Very promising," Zinga replied promptly.

"It's plain we can't keep on squatting here forever," mused the ranger from dusky Falthar. "I'd vote to strip the ship, take everything we can possibly use, and establish a base. Then look around a bit—"

"Fylh?"

The Trystian's claws beat a tattoo on his broad belt. "I agree with that wholly. But it's probably too sensible." His half-sneered ending appeared to be directed at Smitt. Fylh was not going to forget in a hurry the old division between ranger and Patrol crewman.

"Zinga?"

"Establish a base, yes. I would say close to that river which houses those delectable creatures. A fine mess of them right now—" His eyelids dropped in mock ecstasy.

Kartr looked at Smitt. "My vote goes with theirs. We have one usable sled left. On it we could ferry the Commander, Mirion and the supplies. If we plunder the main drive we should be able to fuel it for a number of trips. The rest of us can walk out, and pack stuff on our backs besides. The land is good, there's food and water to be found—and it seems to be deserted—no evidence of anything like the Greenies to fight us for it. If I were the Commander—"

"But you aren't—you Bemmy ranger—you aren't!"

Kartr's hand had fallen to the grip of his hand blaster even before he saw the man who was edging through the door. The wave of menace which he emitted was like a physical blow to the ranger's sensitive perception.

Knowing that any answer he might make verbally would only feed the other's rage, Kartr hesitated, and in the moment of silence Smitt took up the challenge.

"Shut up, Snyn!"

Light glinted from the small weapon almost completely concealed in the armsman's hand as he turned it toward the com-techneer. The waves of fear-based hatred were so thick that Kartr marveled that the others could not feel them too. Without attempting to gain his feet the sergeant hurled himself sideways, his shoulder catching Snyn at knee height. A bolt of searing green flame cut high through the air as the armsman's trigger finger tightened convulsively. He staggered forward as Kartr tried in vain to use his one good hand to pull him off balance.

A second or two later and it was over. Snyn still rolled and screamed muffled curses under Zinga but Fylh was methodically forcing his arms behind him so that a "safe" bar might be locked across his wrists. That done he was pushed over on his back and settled into position for questioning, with jerks which were anything but gentle.

"He's crazy!" Smitt stated with honest conviction. "Using a hand blaster like that. What in Black Heaven—!"

"I should have burned you all—" mouthed the captive. "Always knew you ranger devils couldn't be trusted. Bemmys—all of you!"

But his stark hatred was more than three-quarters fear. Kartr sank down on the bedroll and regarded the twisting man with startled concern. He had known that the rangers were not accepted as full members of the Patrol, he also knew that there was a growing prejudice against nonhuman races—the "Bemmys"—but this raw and frightening rage directed by a crewman against his own shipmates was worse than anything he had ever dreamed possible.

"We have done nothing against you, Snyn—"

The armsman spat. And Kartr guessed that he could not reach him with any reasoning. There was only one thing left to do. But it was something he had sworn to himself long ago never to try—not against any of his own kind. And would the others allow him if he wished to? He stared across the writhing body of the armsman at Smitt.

"He's dangerous—"

Smitt glanced up at the ragged tear in the wall, still glowing cherry red.

"You don't have to underline that!" Then the comtechneer shifted his feet uneasily. "What are you going to do with him?"

Long afterward Kartr realized that that had been the turning point. For, instead of appealing to Smitt or to his own men for backing, he made his own decision. Lightning swift and compelling he launched his will against the guard of the man before him. Snyn's contorted face was a dusky red, his twisted mouth flecked with foam. But he had no control, no mind barrier which could hold against the sergeant's trained power. His eyes glazed, fixed. He ceased to struggle, his mouth fell slackly open.

Smitt half drew his own blaster.

"What are you doing to him?"

Snyn was relaxed and very still now, his eyes on the metal above him.

Smitt reached out to clutch at Kartr's shoulder. "What did you do to him?"

"Quieted him down. He'll sleep it off."

But Smitt was edging toward the door, backing out. "Let me alone!" His voice rose shakily. "Let me alone—you—you blasted Bemmy!" He scrambled for the opening in panicky haste but Rolth reached it before him to block his exit. Smitt turned and faced them, breathing hard—a hunted animal.

"We're not going to touch you." Kartr did not move

44

from his seat or raise his voice. Rolth caught the hand signal he made. The Faltharian hesitated a second and then he obeyed, stepping out of the doorway. But even seeing a clear exit now Smitt did not move. Instead he continued to watch Kartr and asked shakily:

"Can you do—do that to any of us?"

"Probably. You have never cultivated a high mind block—any of you."

Smitt's blaster went back into its holster. He rubbed his sweating face with trembling hands.

"Then why didn't you—just now—?"

"Why didn't I use the mind power on you? Why should I? You weren't planning to burn us—you were entirely sane—"

Smitt was steadying. The panic which had ridden him was almost gone. Reason controlled emotion. He came forward and peered down at the sleeping armsman.

"How long will he be like this?"

"I have no way of knowing. I have never used this on a human being before."

Awe overrode the other's personal fear.

"And you can knock us all out like that?"

"With a man of greater self-control or strong will, it would be a harder task. Then they have to be tricked into dropping their mind guards. But Snyn had no guards up at all."

"That," Zinga said smoothly, "is not going to be your way out of this, Smitt. If you are planning to have the sergeant go around and drop all the opposition in their tracks you can just forget it. We will either reason it out with them or—"

But Smitt was already aware of the next point. "We fight?" he asked almost grimly. "But that will be—"

"Mutiny? Of course, my dear sir. However, if you had not had that in your mind all along you would not have come to us, would you?" Fylh demanded.

Mutiny! Kartr made himself consider it calmly. In space or on planet Vibor was the Commander of the *Starfire*. And every man aboard had once sworn an oath to obey his orders and uphold the authority of the Service. Tork, realizing the officer's condition, might have removed Vibor. But Tork was gone and not one man aboard the ship now had the legal right to set aside the Commander's orders. The sergeant got to his feet.

"Can you get Jaksan and Dalgre—"

He looked about the rangers' quarters. No, it would be wiser to hold a meeting in some more neutral place. Outside, he decided swiftly, where the psychological effect of the ruined ship right before their eyes all during the discussion might well be the deciding point.

"Outside?" he ended.

"All right," agreed Smitt, but there was a note of reluctance in that. He went out.

"Now," Zinga asked, after watching the com-techneer safely out of hearing range, "what are we in for?"

"This would have come sooner or later anyway—it was inevitable after the crash." That was Rolth's soft voice answering. "When we were space borne, they had a reason for life—they could close their eyes and minds to things, drugging themselves with a round of familiar duties. Now that has been swept away from them. We are the ones who have a purpose—a job. And because we are—different—we have always been slightly suspect—"

"So," Kartr put into words the thought which had been growing in his own mind, "unless we act and give them something to work for, *we* may become the target for their fear and resentment? I agree."

"We could cut loose," Fylh suggested. "When the ship crashed our ties with her were broken. Records—who's ever going to see any of our records now? We're able to live off the land—"

"But they might not be able to," Kartr pointed out.

"And it is just because that is true that we can't cut loose and go. Not now anyway. We shall have to try and help them—"

Zinga laughed. "Always the idealist, Kartr. I'm a Bemmy, Fylh's a Bemmy, Rolth's half Bemmy and you're a Bemmy lover and we're all rangers, which in no way endears any of us to these so-called human Patrolmen. All right, we'll try to make them see the light. But I'll do my arguing with a blaster near my hand."

Kartr did not demur. After the resentment with which Jaksan had greeted him when they returned from the trip and the insane attack of Snyn, he knew enough to understand that such preparedness on their part was necessary.

"Do we count on Smitt, I wonder," Zinga mused. "He never before impressed me as a ranger recruit."

"No, but he does have brains," Rolth pointed out. "Kartr"—he turned to the sergeant—"it will be your play—we'll let you do the talking now."

The other two nodded. Kartr smiled. Inside him was a good warm feeling. He had known it before—the rangers stood together. Come what might, they were going to present a united front to danger.

Together the four rangers crossed the ground burnt off by the ship's rockets to stand partially in the shadow of a tall rock outcrop. The sun was far down now—sending red and yellow spears of light up the western sky. But its day heat still radiated from both sand and stone.

Jaksan, Dalgre and Smitt awaited them, eyes narrowed against the light reflected from the metal of the *Starfire*—standing close together as if they were expecting—what? Attack? There were grim lines about the mouth of the arms officer. He was middle-aged, but always before there had been an elasticity in his movements, an alertness in his voice and manner which had given the lie to the broad sweeps of gray hair showing on his temples. In the golden days of the Service, Kartr realized with a slight shock of surprise, Jaksan would not have been in space at all. Long since, regulations would have retired him to some administrative post in one of the fleet ports. Did the Patrol still have any such ports? Kartr himself had not earthed in one for at least five years now.

"Well, what do you want with us?" Jaksan took the initiative.

But Kartr refused to be in any way impressed or intimidated. "It is necessary"—by instinct he fell back into the formal speech he had heard in his childhood—"for us

48

to consider now the future. Look at the ship—" He did not need to wave his hand toward that shattered bulk. They had, none of them, been able to keep their eyes away from it. "Can you truly think that it shall ever lift again? We began this last flight undersupplied. And those supplies we have drawn upon now for months—they must be almost gone. There remains but one thing for us to do—we must strip the ship and establish a camp on the land—"

"That is just the sort of jap we expected to hear out of you!" snapped Dalgre. "You are still under orders—whether we have crashed or not!"

But it wasn't Jaksan who had made the hot retort. Jaksan was steeped, buried in the Patrol, in orders, in tradition—but he was not blinded or deafened by it.

"Whose orders?" asked Kartr now. "The Commander is incapacitated. Are you in command now, sir?" He addressed Jaksan directly.

The arms officer's space-burned skin could not pale, but his face was drawn and old. His lips drew back from his teeth in an animal's snarl of rage, pain and frustration. Before he answered he stared again at the broken ship.

"This will kill Vigor—" He bit out the words one by one.

Kartr braced himself as the wild emotion of the other tore at his perceptive sense. He could still Jaksan's pain by joining the other—by refusing to believe that the old life was ended and gone. Perhaps the Service had warped them all, the rangers as well as the crew, perhaps they needed the reassurance of orders, of routine—even going through the forms might be an anchor now.

The sergeant saluted. "Have I your permission to prepare to abandon ship, sir?"

For a moment he tensed as Jaksan whirled upon him. But the arms officer did not reach for a blaster. Instead his shoulders hunched, the lines in his face deepened into gashes of pain.

"Do as you please!" Then he strode away from them, behind the rocks and no one moved to follow him.

Kartr took command. "Zinga, Rolth, get out the sled and two days' supplies. Raid the main drive for fuel. Then go up and establish a base below the falls. You bring the sled back, Rolth, and we'll send along the Commander and Mirion—"

They ate an unpalatable meal of rations, and went to work. Some time later Jaksan was back among them to labor doggedly without speech. Kartr thankfully surrendered to him the responsibility of gathering the arms and the crew's supplies. The rangers kept away from the crewmen—there was plenty to do in stripping their own quarters and breaking out all the exploring gear the *Starfire* had ever carried. Piloted by Rolth, to whom the darkness was as bright as day, the sled made three trips during the night, taking the injured and the still unconscious Snyn as well as supplies of salvage.

A moon, a single one, rose to hang in the night sky. They were glad of its light to eke out the short line of their small portable lamps. They worked, with brief periods of rest, until the gray of dawn made a rim about the desert. It was in that last hour of labor that Jaksan made the most promising find. He had crawled alone into the crushed drive room and then shouted loud enough to bring them, numb with fatigue, hurrying to him.

Fuel—a whole extra tube of cubes! They stared round-eyed as the arms officer dragged it out into the passageway.

"Save it," Jaksan panted. "We may need the use of the sled badly later—"

Kartr, remembering the height of the falls cliffs, nodded.

So it was, that in spite of their find, when Rolth came

back the next time they loaded the tube on the sled but gave him orders not to return. They would eat, sleep away the heat of the coming day, and make the trip on foot, packing their personal possessions on their backs.

The sun was shining when they gathered together in a little group by the rocks. And a blue-black shadow cast by the wrecked ship fell on three mounds in the sand. Jaksan read with parched lips and a stumbling tongue the old words of the Service farewell. They would erect no monument—until the years wore her remains into red dust the *Starfire* would mount guard above her crewmen.

After that they slept soddenly, for the last time, in the stripped ship. Fylh shook Kartr awake after what seemed only a moment's rest—but it was close to sunset. The sergeant choked down dry scraps of ration with the others. Then together, without much talk, they settled their packs and set out across the wedge of desert, steering by rock formations Kartr had noted the day before.

It was soon night again, lighted by a full moon, and they did not turn on the hand lamps. Which was just as well, thought the sergeant grimly, as there was no hope of ever renewing the fire units in those. Since they were not trying to follow the river, but cutting cross country by the route the sled had followed on its first return, they came out on that smooth section of roadway. Kartr called it to Jaksan's attention.

"Road!" For the first time the arms officer was lifted out of his depression. He went down on his knees to pass his hands over the ancient blocks, snapping on his torch to see the better. "Not much of it showing. It must have been here a long, long time. Could you trace it—?"

"With the tailer on the sled, yes. But with fuel so low—would it be worth it?"

Jaksan got wearily to his feet again. "I don't know. We can keep that in mind. It could be a lead, but I don't know—" He lapsed into a deep study as they moved on but at the next halt he spoke with some of his old fire. "Dalgre, what was that process you told me about—the one for adapting disruptor shells for power?"

His assistant armsman looked up eagerly.

"It is—" Within three words he had plunged into a flood of technicalities which left the rangers as far behind as if he were speaking some tongue from another galaxy. The *Starfire* might have lacked a mech-techneer, but Jaksan was an expert in his field and he had seen that his juniors knew more than just the bare essentials of their craft. Dalgre was still pouring out his explanation when they moved on and the arms officer walked beside him listening, now and then shooting a question which set the younger man's tongue to racing again.

They did not make the lift up the cliff to the plains country at once. Mirion died three days later, to be buried in a small clearing between two of the tall pointed trees. Fylh and Zinga rolled a sizable boulder from the river's edge and Rolth used a palm disrupter as lightly as a color brush to etch into its side the name, home world, and the rank of that thin wasted body they had laid to rest there.

Vibor never spoke. He ate mechanically, or rather chewed and swallowed what Jaksan or Smitt put into his mouth. He slept most of the time and showed no interest in what went on about him. The old division between rangers and crew, between the regulars and the less strictly disciplined specialists, was slowly closing as they worked together, hunted together, ate of unfamiliar flesh, nuts and berries. So far their immunity shots continued to work—or else they had not sampled anything poisonous.

The morning after Mirion's burial Kartr suggested that they go up into the more hospitable country behind the falls. Jaksan raised no objection and they lifted their supplies via the sled to a point about a mile up and farther ahead of their first base. From there Fylh took the sled with Vibor and Jaksan as passengers toward the promise

52

of open country, while the others cached such equipment as they could not pack and started to follow overland.

Zinga splashed first through the flood pools along the rocky shore of the river—the leader because he had two hands to Kartr's one. The sergeant followed behind with Dalgre, Snyn, and Smitt strung out in his wake and Rolth bringing up the rear to discourage straggling. There was a sweetness in the morning air. It was chill enough to prickle the flesh, but it bore with it scents which promised and pleased. Kartr lifted his head to the touch of the wind, drawing it deeply into his lungs. The smog of the *Starfire* was very far in the past. He discovered that he had few regrets for its loss. What if they *were* exiled here for life—just to find such a world was luck enough!

He sent out his sense of perception, blanking out the touches of those about him—trying to make contact with a native life. A reddish animal with a pouf of tail escorted them for a space, traveling high in tree limbs, making a chattering noise. It was only curious—curious and totally unafraid.

A bird—or maybe it was some form of insect—sailed through the air, coasting on wings which were brilliant patches of color. Then another animal trotted out of concealment perhaps a hundred feet ahead of their line of march. It was large—almost as formidable in size as the brown-coated fisher they had seen on their first day. But this one's fur was a tawny yellow-brown and it moved shadow-silent, slipping across the rocks with surety and arrogance. It crouched, belly close to the gray stone, and watched them through slitted dark eyes. The tip of its tail twitched. Zinga stopped to allow Kartr to join him.

Arrogance—arrogance and curiosity—and the faint stirrings of hunger, no thread of fear or wariness. The beast was beginning to consider them as food—

Kartr studied it, saw the muscles ripple under the thick fur as it moved slowly forward. It was beautiful—so wonderful in its wild freedom that he wanted to know more of it. He made contact, felt his way into that alien brain.

The hunger was there, but at his touch it began to submerge—the curiosity was stronger. It sat up, front limbs straight, haunches tucked in. Only the twitching tail tip betrayed its slight unease.

Without turning his head Kartr gave an order. "March to the left a bit—angle around the rock there. It will not attack us now—"

"Why don't you just blast it?" demanded Snyn querulously. "All this stupid 'don't kill this—don't kill that'! The thing's only an animal after all—"

"Shut up!" Smitt gave the crewman a slight push to set him going. "Don't try to teach a ranger his business. Remember, if they hadn't made contact with those purple jelly flying things we wouldn't have come through the Greenie attack—those devils would have wiped us out without warning."

Snyn grunted, but he turned to the left. Smitt, Dalgre and Rolth followed—Zinga went last of all. Kartr remained until the last of the party had passed the forest beast. It yawned abruptly, displaying wicked fangs. Then, almost sleepy-eyed, it sat there, statue still, to watch them out of sight. Kartr brought up the rear. The creature was in two minds about following them. Curiosity pulled it after the travelers, hunger suggested the more immediate employment of hunting. And, at last, hunger won, the sergeant's contact faded as the animal slipped back into the woodland, away from their path.

But the meeting left Kartr both puzzled and faintly disturbed. He had made contact easily enough—had been able to impress the animal properly with the idea that they were not food and that they meant no harm. But he had been totally unsuccessful in his attempt to establish any closer relationship. Here was certainly nothing like the purple jelly thing, nothing which could be counted upon to render aid to man. The forest animal had a wild and fierce independence which refused the command of his will. If all the natives of this world were so conditioned it would leave the handful of shipwrecked survivors just that much more isolated and alone.

Man, or at least superior life form of some type—or they wouldn't have constructed a road on which to travel—had once lived here. They had been here a long time and in some numbers—or that road would not run through the edge of wastelands. And yet no living creature he had so far encountered had any memory, or even an instinctive fear, of man. How long had the race who build that road been gone—where had they gone—and why? He longed to take off with the sled and the tailer and run along the road which could never be buried so deeply that the pointer could not betray it—run along it to the city which must lie somewhere near its end or beginning.

Cities—cities were mostly found along the edges of continental land masses where there were opportunities of sea travel—or in strategic points by river beds. There were seas on this planet—he mourned again in silence the crushing of the pilot's recorder which had rendered useless the notations made as they had come in to that fatal landing. Maybe if they struck due east now—or west—they would come out upon the sea coast. Only which way—east or west? He had had only one fleeting glimpse at the ship's viewplate and it had appeared that the land mass they had set down upon had been a very large one. They might be hundreds of planet miles from either coast. Would even that road be the right guide?

Once they had a good base established he was going, Kartr promised himself, to get to the bottom of the fuel source Dalgre and Jaksan had been talking about. With the sled repowered they could explore much farther than they could hope to do on foot. And with the road as a beginning—

Rolth had come to a full stop and was looking back.

"You are happy?"

Kartr realized that he had been humming.

"I was thinking about that road—of following it—"

"Yes—it sticks in one's mind—that road. But what good would it be to us? Do you honestly believe that we shall find man—or even man's distant kindred—at the end of it?"

"I don't know—"

"That, of course"—Rolth wriggled his shoulders to settle his pack the better—"is my true answer. What we do not know, we must find out— It is that urge to go and see what lies beyond the hills which brought us into the rangers. We are conditioned to such searching. I must admit that I would relish such an expedition much more than I do this crawling from place to place through a wilderness, bending under burdens as if I were a draft pfph from the outer islands of Falthar!"

It took them almost two full days of tramping to reach the camp Fylh and Jaksan had made. But once there they found waiting them shelters constructed from tree branches, a fire going to light them in through the dusk of evening, and the savor of roasting meat to turn their tired shuffle into strides again.

A shelf of rock ran down smoothly into the shallows of the stream, offering a natural landing place for the sled. At the back of this was piled the material ferried up the river. Jaksan had located some wild grain, fully ripe, and some sourish fruit from trees growing at the edge of the woods. A man would have no difficulty living off the land here, Kartr decided. He wondered about the seasons— whether there was any great change between them during the years. Not to know—not to have any guides! Seasons had not mattered when they were only visitors in a strange world—but now— There was so much they should know—and would have to learn by the hard way of experience.

He stretched out by the fire, trying to list all that should be done—so deep in his thought that he was honestly startled when Rolth touched his shoulder. The night world was Rolth's and he was alive with it as were the beasts now prowling beyond the circle of the firelight.

"Come!" The urgency in that one whispered word got Kartr to his feet. He gave a quick glance about the fire. The rest were in their bedrolls, asleep, or putting on a good show of being so. The sergeant crept out of the light, not setting his full foot to the ground until he reached the shadows.

"What—?" But he did not get to complete that question. Rolth's hand was on his arm and the fingers pressed into his flesh in a warning.

Then those fingers slipped down until they tightened about his and Rolth drew him on into the full dark.

They were going up a slope which steepened as they advanced. The trees thinned out and vanished, leaving them in the moonlit open. On the crown of the hill the Faltharian pulled the sergeant around to face north.

"Wait!" Rolth ordered tersely. "Watch the sky!"

Kartr blinked into the curtain of the night. It was a clear one, stars made familiar and unfamiliar patterns across the sky. He remembered other suns and the myriad worlds they nourished.

Across the horizon from left to right swept a yellow-white beam, reaching from some point on the earth ahead far into the heavens. It took three seconds for it to complete the full sweep. Kartr counted. Sixty seconds later it leaped into sight once more, moving in the same course. A beacon!

"How long—?"

"I saw it first an hour ago. It is very regular."

"It must be a beacon, a marker—but for whom—run by whom—?"

"Must it be run by anyone?" asked Rolth thoughtfully. "Remember Tantor—"

Tantor, the sealed city. Its inhabitants had been overwhelmed by a ghastly plague two centuries ago. Yes, he recalled Tantor well. Once he had flown above the vast bubble which enclosed it in an eternal prison for the safety of the galaxy, and had watched the ancient machines going about their business below, running a city in which no living thing walked or ever would walk again. Tantor had had its beacons too, and its appeals for help streaming into the skies mechanically long after the hands which had set them going had been dust. Behind those hills ahead might well rest another Tantor—it would explain the puzzle of a fair but deserted world.

"Ask Jaksan to come," Kartr said at last. "But do not arouse the others."

Rolth disappeared and the sergeant stood alone, watching the light sweep across the sky in its timed sequence. Was the machine which cast that tended or untended? Was that some signal for help, a help long since unneeded? Was it a guide set for a ship from the stars which had never arrived?

He heard the roll of loose gravel started by an impatient foot. The arms officer was on his way.

"What is it?" Jaksan demanded impatiently a moment later.

Kartr did not turn around. "Look due north," he ordered. "See that!"

The beam made the arc across the horizon. Kartr heard a gasp which was almost a cry.

"It must be a signal of some sort," the sergeant continued. "And I would judge mechanically broadcast—"

"From a city!" Jaksan added eagerly.

"Or a landing port. But—remember Tantor?"

The other's silence was his answer.

"What do you propose to do?" Jaksan asked after a long moment.

"This process you were discussing with Dalgre—can you use disruptor charges in the sled? We must keep the extra fuel for emergencies."

"We can try to do it. It was done once and Dalgre read the report. Suppose we can—what then?"

"I'll take the sled and investigate that."

"Alone?"

Kartr shrugged. "With not more than one other. If that is a dead monument, another Tantor, we dare not be too precipitant in exploration. And the fewer to risk their necks the better."

The arms officer chewed on that. Again the touch of resentment he could not altogether keep under reached Kartr. He guessed what the other must be feeling now. That signal ahead might mean at the very best a star port, a chance to find another still navigable ship, to return to the safe familiar life the Patrol officer had always known. At the very least it promised remains of a civilization of sorts, if only a pile of ruins which could be used to shelter men against the raw life of a wilderness world.

It was up to the rangers to be patient with such men as Jaksan. What to them was a promise of a free and proper way of life was to these unwilling companions of theirs a slipping back into utter darkness. If Jaksan would give way entirely to his emotions now he would rush madly for the sled, and ride it toward the beacon. But he kept that desire under stiff curb, he was no Snyn.

"We go to work on the sled at dawn," the arms officer promised. "No," as Kartr started down the hill and he did not move to follow, "I shall stay here a little while longer."

Well, Rolth was making the rounds as night guard. He would see that Jaksan came to no harm. Kartr went back to the fire alone. Crawling into his bedroll he closed his eyes and willed himself to sleep. But in his dreams a thrust of yellow-white light both threatened and beckoned.

Jaksan was as good as his word. The next morning Dalgre, Snyn and the arms officer dismantled the largest of the disruptors and gingerly worked loose its power unit. Because they were handling sudden and violent death they worked slowly, testing each relay and installation over and over again. It took a full day of painful work on the sled before they were through, and even then they could not be sure it would really rise.

Just before sunset Fylh took the pilot's seat, getting in as if he didn't altogether care for his place just over those tinkered-with power units. But he had insisted upon playing test pilot.

The sled went up with a lurch, too strong a surge. Then it straightened out neatly, as Fylh learned how to make adjustments, and sped across the river, to circle and return, alighting with usual care considering who had the controls. Fylh spoke to Jaksan before he was off his seat.

"She has a lot more power than she had before. How long is it going to last?"

Jaksan rubbed a grimy hand across his forehead. "We have no way of telling. What did that report say, Dalgre?"

"The Mona hook-up brought a cruiser in three light years to base. Then they dug it out. They never learned how long it might have lasted."

Fylh nodded and turned to Kartr.

"Well, she's ready and waiting. When do we take off, sergeant?"

# 5

# THE CITY

In the end the rangers drew lots for the pilot's place and the choice fell, not to Fylh, but to Rolth. Secretly Kartr was pleased. To fly with Rolth at the controls would mean going by night—but that would be the wiser thing to do when covering a strange city. And, after all, Rolth had been the one to discover the beacon.

They set off at dusk, rations and bedrolls strapped under the single seat remaining in the stripped-down sled. And with the bedrolls was the single disruptor they had left. Jaksan had insisted upon their taking that.

Rolth sang softly as they sped through the chill of the dusk—one of the minor wailing airs of his own twilight world. Without his protective goggles his dark eyes were alive in his pallid face.

Kartr leaned back against the seat pad and watched the ground darken from green to dusky blue. Just on chance he triggered the tailer. Now if they did pass above any large man-made object they would be warned.

There was life abroad in the hills below—animal hunters on the prowl. And once a wild screech reached them. Kartr read in that sound the rage and the disgust of a hunter that had missed its spring and must stalk again. But no man walked below them—nothing even close to human.

The tailer clicked. Kartr leaned forward and consulted the dial. One point only. And a small one. But—manmade. A single building perhaps—maybe long buried. Not the site of the beacon.

Even as he thought of it the beam swept across the dusk-darkened sky. No, whatever lay below had no connection with that.

There were hills and more hills. Rolth applied power which raised them over, sometimes hardly skimming above rocks which crowned the peaks. Then they began to drop away again, making steps for a giant down into another low land.

And now they could see what lay in the heart of that. A blaze of light, not all yellow-white, but emerald, ruby, sapphire too! A handful of gigantic gems spilled out to pulse and glow in the night.

Kartr had visited the elfin ruins of lost Calinn—needle towers and iridescent domes—a city no man living in the days of human civilization could duplicate. He had seen sealed Tantor, and the famous City of the Sea, built of stone-encased living organisms beneath the waters of Parth. But this—it was queerly familiar as well as alien. He was drawn and repelled by it at the same time.

He put a hand to the controls to give Rolth a chance to resume his goggles. What was bright light for the sergeant was blinding to the Faltharian.

"Do we just fly in—or scout first?" asked Rolth.

Kartr frowned, sending his perceptive sense ahead—a surgeon's delicate probe, prying into the source of the lights.

He touched what he sought, touched and recoiled in the same instant, fleeing the awareness of the mind he had contacted. But what he had found was so astounding that he was too startled to answer that question at once. When he did it was decisively.

"We scout—!"

Rolth cut down the speed of the sled. He swung it out in an arc to encircle the splotch of light.

"I wouldn't have believed it!" Kartr gave voice at last to his bewilderment.

"There are inhabitants?"

"One at least—I contacted an Arcturus Three mind!"

"Pirates?" suggested Rolth.

"In an open city—with all that light to betray them? Though, you may be right at that, that is just where they might feel safe. But be careful, we don't want to walk straight into a blast beam. And that kind fire before they ask your name and planet—especially if they see our Comets!"

"Did he catch your mind touch?"

"Who knows what an Arcturian gets or doesn't get? No one has been able to examine them unless they are either completely unaware or deliberately open. He could have been either then."

"More than one?"

"I got out—fast—when I tapped him. Didn't stay to see."

The tailer was clicking madly. Kartr should have switched on the recorder, too. But without a machine to read the wire that was useless. From now on scouting reports would be oral. The sled glided slowly over a section where the buildings stood some distance apart, vegetation thick between them.

"Look—" Rolth pointed to the left. "That's a landing stage there—if I ever saw one. How about setting down on the next one and going ahead on foot—"

"Get in closer to the main part of the city first. No use in walking several miles after we go down."

They found what they wanted, a small landing stage on the top of a tower, a tower which seemed short when compared to the buildings around it, though they must have landed forty floors above street level. But it was a good place from which to spy out the land.

They dropped on it. Then Kartr whirled, his blaster out—aimed for the middle of the black thing scuttling toward him from the roof shadows. He tried in the same instant for mind contact—to recoil with an instant of real panic. And Rolth put his discovery into words.

"Robot—guard—maybe—"

Kartr was back in the sled as Rolth brought it up above the head of the figure.

Robot, guard or attendant, the thing stopped short when the sled left the stage surface. As they went on up it turned squarely and trundled away into the dark. Kartr relaxed. The metal guardian could have beamed them both before they had even had a chance to sight it. Of course, it might only have been an attendant—but there was no sense in taking the risk.

"No more landing stages," he said and Rolth agreed with him fervently.

"Those creatures might be conditioned to a voice or a key word—give them the wrong answer and they take you apart quick—"

"Wait a minute." Kartr put his blaster back in its holster. "We're judging this city by what we know of our own civilization." He squinted against the brilliance of a wave of green light and recited the instructions of their manual, "There is always something new for the finder, go out with an open mind—"

"And," Rolth added, "a ready blaster! Yes, I know all that. But human nature remains the same and I'd rather be wary than dead. Look down there—see those squares of pavement between the buildings? How about setting down on one of those? No landing stage alarms or controls we could trigger—"

"Promising. Can you get in behind that big block? Its shadow should hide us well—"

64

Rolth might not get as much speed out of the sled as Fylh did, but his caution on such a mission as this was more to be desired than the Trystian's reckless disregard for the laws of gravity. Earthing required of him a good five minutes of painful maneuvering, but he brought them down in the middle of the pool of shadow Kartr had indicated.

They did not stir from their seats at once, but sat watching for robots, for any moving thing which might promise menace.

"A city"—Rolth stated the obvious—"is not place to play hide and seek in. I'm sure that I'm being watched— maybe from up there—" He jerked a thumb at the lines of blank windows overlooking the court in which they had landed.

That eerie sensation—that myriad eyes were peering hostilely from the blank expanses—Kartr knew it too. But his sense told him it was a lie.

"Nothing living here," he assured the Faltharian. "Not even a robot."

They moved away from the sled, skirting the side of the nearest building, staying in the shadows, racing across lighted open spaces. Rolth ran his fingers along the wall at his shoulder. "Old, very old. I can feel the scars of erosion."

"But the lights? How long could those keep running?" wondered Kartr.

"Ask your friend from Arcturus. Maybe he put them in working order when he arrived. Who knows?"

There was little ornamentation on the buildings they passed, the walls were smoothly functional, yet the very way the towers and blocks were fitted into a harmonious whole argued that they were the product of a civilization so advanced in architecture as to present a city as a unit, instead of a collection of buildings and dwellings of individuals tastes and periods. So far Kartr had seen no inscriptions on any of the structures.

Rolth's blue torch flashed on and off regularly as they went, pin-dotting their trail through this new kind of wilderness. When they wanted to retrace their way he need only touch his light again on these walls and the tiny blue circles would glow in return for a second.

The rangers made a half circle around one of the three buildings hedging in the court and crept along a street into the surface of which their feet sank almost ankle deep. The old pavement was covered with a thick growth of short tough grass. Half a block ahead, from a recess between two buildings, a rainbow of light played. They approached it cautiously—to come upon a fountain, a fountain of plumed light as well as tinkling water. The flood it raised sank back into a round basin, the rim of which was broken on the side near them so that a small stream was free to cut a channel through the sod until it reached a hole in the ancient pavement.

"No one around," Kartr whispered. Why he whispered he could not have explained. But the feeling of being watched, of being followed, persisted. Beneath the shadow of these dead towers he felt it necessary to creep and crawl silently—unless he awaken—what?

They dared to leave the protection of the dark and come out to the edge of the fountain. Now, through the spray of water and light, they could see its center column. There was a figure on it—more than life size, unless the builders of the city had been giants. It was not of any stone they could recognize but some white, gleaming stuff upon which time had left no marks. And, at the full sight of it, both Kartr and Rolth stopped almost in midstride.

A girl stood there—her arms above her head, with a mane of unbound hair flowing free below her slender waist. In her upheld hands she grasped a symbol they both knew—a star of five points. And it was from the tips

66

of those points that the water gushed. But the girl—she was no Bemmy—she was as human as they.

"It's Ionate—the Spirit of the Spring Rain—" Kartr reached far into his mind and drew forth a legend of his blasted home.

"No—it's Xyti of the Frosts!" Rolth had memories, too, stemming from his own dusky world of cold and shadow.

For a second they stared at each other almost angrily and then both smiled.

"She is both—and neither—" Rolth suggested. "These men had their spirits of beauty, too. But it is plain by her eyes and hair she is not of Falthar. And by her ears—she is no kin of yours—"

"But why—" Kartr stared at the fountain in puzzlement. "Why does she seem as if I have known her always? And that star—"

"A common symbol—you have seen it a hundred times on a hundred different worlds. No, it is as I have said. She is the ideal of beauty and so we see her, even as he who fashioned her dreamed her into being."

They left the court of the fountain reluctantly and came into a wide avenue which stretched its green length straight toward the center of the city. Now and again colored lights formed untranslatable signs in the air or across the fronts of the buildings. They passed by what must have been shops and saw the cobwebs of ancient wares spread inside the windows. Then Kartr caught Rolth's arm and pulled him quickly into the shelter of a doorway.

"Robot!" The sergeant's lips were close to his companion's ear. "I think it is patrolling!"

"Can we circuit it?"

"Depends upon its type."

They had only their past experience to guide them. The robot patrols, they knew, were deadly danger. Those they had seen elsewhere could not be turned from duty except by the delicate and dangerous act of short circuiting their controls. Otherwise the robot would either blast without question anything or anyone not natural to that place or who could not answer it with the prescribed code. It was what the rangers had feared on the landing stage, and it would be even worse to face it now when they had no sled for a quick getaway.

"It will depend upon whether this is a native or—"

"Or introduced by the Arcturian?" Rolth interrupted. "Yes, if he brought it, we know how to handle it. A native—"

He stopped whispering at the faint sound of metal clinking against stone. Kartr straightened and flashed his torch above their heads. The doorway in which they crouched was not too high and a small projection overhung it. Just over that was the dark break of a window. Seeing that he began to plan.

"Inside—" he said to Rolth. "Try to reach the second floor and get out of that window upon the ledge. Then I'll attract the robot's attention and you can burn its brain case from above—"

Rolth was gone, slipping into the darkness which was no barrier to him. Kartr leaned against the side of the doorway. It would be a race, he thought, with a little sick twinge in the pit of his stomach. If the robot got here before Rolth reached that ledge—! If he, Kartr, couldn't manage to avoid the first attack of the patroller—! Luckily he didn't have too long to wait and catalogue all those dismal possibilities.

He could see the patroller now. It was at the far end of the block. The flashing lights on the buildings played across its metal body. But the sergeant was almost sure that it was unlike the ones known to galactic cities. The rounded dome of the head casing, the spider-like slenderness of the limbs, the almost graceful smoothness of its progress, were akin more to the architecture of this place.

Its pace was steady and unhurried. It paused before each doorway and shot a spy beam from its head into the entrance. Manifestly it was going about its appointed task of checking the security of each portal.

Then the sergeant sighed with relief. Rolth had crawled into place and crouched now well above the line of the robot's vision. If only this patroller was constructed on the same general pattern they knew and *could* be short circuited through the head!

But when it reached the next doorway it hesitated. Kartr tensed. This might be worse than he had thought. The thing had some sense perception. He was sure that it suspected his presence. No spy beam flashed. Instead it stood there unmoving—as if it were puzzled, making up its mind.

Was it relaying back to some dust-covered headquarters an alarm?

But its arms were moving—

"Kartr!"

Night sight or no night sight, Kartr had not needed that shout from Rolth to warn him. He had already seen what the patroller held ready. He hurled himself backward, falling flat on the floor of the hall, letting momentum carry him in a slide some distance along it. Behind him was a burst of eye-searing flame, filling the whole entrance with an inferno. Only his trained muscles and sixth sense of preservation had saved him from cooking in the midst of that!

Shakily he crawled on his belly away from the holocaust. Was the robot going to follow him in and complete its mission?

Hollow sounds of feet pounding—

"Kartr! Kartr!"

He had levered himself to a sitting position when Rolth

plunged around an angle in the hallway and almost fell over him.

"Are you hurt? Did he get you?"

Kartr grinned lopsidedly. To just be alive—he winced as Rolth's examining hands touched skin scraped raw.

"What about—?"

"The bag of bolts? I scragged him all right—a blast hole right through his head casing and he went down. He didn't reach you?"

"No. And at least he's told us something about the civilization they had here. They were still using atomics." The sergeant surveyed the blaze behind him with critical distaste. "Blow a hole in a city block to get someone. Wonder what they would have thought of a stun gun." With Rolth's hand under his arm Kartr got to his feet. He hoped that he had not rebroken his wrist and that the red agony in it was only from the jar of his fall.

"I have a feeling," he began and then was glad that Rolth had retained a grip on him because the hallway appeared to sway under his feet, "that we'd better get away from here—fast—"

The thought which plagued him was the memory of that momentary pause before the robot had attacked. Kartr was sure that then a message had been flashed from the patroller—where? If the timeless machine had only been performing rounds set him generations before the city had been deserted by its builder—then such a report would be no menace—unless it activated other machines in turn. On the other hand, if the mysterious Arcturian controlled the robots, then the rangers might have successfully met a first attack, only to face other and perhaps worse ones.

Rolth agreed with this when he suggested it aloud.

"We can't go back that way anyhow." The Faltharian pointed to the blazing pit of radiation which had once been the door. "And they may just be combing the streets for us, too. Listen, this city reminds me in some ways of Stiltu—"

Kartr shook his head. "Heard of it, but have never been there."

"Capital of Lydias I." Rolth identified it impatiently. "They're old-fashioned there—still live in big cities. Well, they have an underground system of links—ways of traveling under the surface—"

"Hm." Kartr's mind jumped to the next point easily. "Then we might try going down and see what we can find? All right. And if that patroller did rouse out the guard before you burned him, it will be some time before they can even get in here to see if their tame hunter bagged us. Let's look for a way down."

But to their bafflement there seemed to be no way down at all. They threaded rooms and halls, pushing past the remains of furnishings and strange machinery which at other times would have set them speculating for hours, hunting some means of descent. None appeared to exist—only two stairways leading up.

In the end they discovered what they wanted in the center of a room. It was a dark well, a black hole in which the beam of Kartr's flash found no end. But if the light did not reveal much it helped them in another way because its owner dropped it. He gave an exclamation and made a futile grab—much too late. Rolth supplied an excited comment, reverting in this stress to his native dialect and only making sense when Kartr demanded harshly that he translate.

"It did not fall! It is floating down—floating!"

The sergeant sat back on his heels. "Inverse descent! Still working!" He could hardly believe that. Small articles might possibly be upborne by the gravity-dispelling rays —but something heavier—a man—say—

Before he could protest Rolth edged over the rim, to dangle by his hands.

"It's working all right! I'm treading air. Here goes!"

His hands disappeared and he was gone. But his voice came up the shaft.

"Still walking on air! Come on in, the swimming's fine!"

Fine for Rolth maybe who could see where he was going. To lower oneself into that black maw and hope that the anti-gravity was *not* going to fail—! Not for the first time in his career with the rangers Kartr silently cursed his overvivid imagination as he allowed his boots to drop into the thin air of the well. He involuntarily closed his eyes and muttered a half-plea to the Spirit of Space as he let go.

But he was floating! The air closed about his body with almost tangible support. He was descending, of course, but at the rate of a feather on a light breeze. Far below he saw the blue light of Rolth's torch. The other had reached bottom. Kartr drew his feet together and tried to aim his body toward the pinprick of light.

"Happy planeting!" Rolth greeted the sergeant as he landed lightly, his knees slightly bent, and with no shock at all. "Come and see what I have found."

What Rolth had found was a platform edging on a tunnel. Anchored to this stand by a slender chain was a small car, pointed at both ends, a single padded seat in its center. It had no drive Kartr could discern and it did not touch the floor of the tunnel, hovering about a foot above that.

A keyboard was just before the seat—controls, Kartr deduced. But how could they aim it to any place? And to go shooting off blindly into the dark, liable to crash against some cave in— The sergeant began to reconsider that—too risky by far. To face a battalion of robot patrollers was less dangerous than to be trapped underground in the dark.

"Here!"

Kartr jumped at Rolth's call. The other ranger had gone to the back of the platform and was holding his dim torch on the wall there. The sergeant could just barely see by the blue light. Rolth had found something all right! A map of black lines crossing and recrossing—it could only be of the tunnel system. Having solved much more complicated puzzles in the past they set to work—to discover that this was apparently a way leading directly into the heart of the city.

Ten minutes later they crowded together on the narrow seat. Rolth pressed two buttons as Kartr threw off the restraining chain. There was a faint puff of sound—they swept forward and the dank air of the tunnel filled their nostrils.

# 6

## THE CITY PEOPLE

"This should be it," Rolth half whispered.

The car was slowing down, drawing to the right side of the tunnel. Ahead a dim light glowed. They must be approaching another platform. Kartr glanced at the dial on his wrist band. It had taken them exactly five minutes planet time to reach this place. Whether or not it was the one they wanted—that was another question. They had aimed at a point they thought would be directly under what seemed to be a large public building in the very center of the city. If any human or Bemmy force had taken over here that would be the logical place to find them.

"Anyone ahead?" asked Rolth, trusting as usual to Kartr's perception.

The sergeant sent a mind probe on and then shook his head. "Not a trace. Either they don't know about these ways or they have no interest in them."

"I'm inclined to believe that they don't know." The Faltharian grabbed at a mooring ring as the car came along the platform.

Kartr climbed out and stood looking about him. This place was at least three times the size of the one from which they had embarked. And other tunnels ran from it in several directions. It was lighted after a fashion. But not brightly enough to make Rolth don his goggles again.

"Now"—the Faltharian stood with his hands resting on his hips, surveying their port—"how do we get out—or rather up—from here?"

There were those other tunnels, but, on their first inspection, no other sign of an exit. Yet Kartr was sure that this platform must have one. It was air which betrayed it—a puff of warmer, less dank breeze which touched him. Rolth must have felt it too for he turned in the direction from which it had come.

They followed that tenuous guide to a flat round plate at the foot of another well. Kartr crooked his neck until his throat strained. Far above he was sure he could see a faint haze of light. But they certainly couldn't climb— He turned to Rolth bitterly disappointed.

"That's that! We might as well go back—"

But the Faltharian was engrossed by a panel of buttons on the wall.

"I don't think we need do that. Let's just see if this works!" He pressed the top button in the row. Then he jumped back to clutch his companion in a tight hold as the plate came to life under them and they zoomed up.

Both rangers instinctively dropped and huddled together. Kartr swallowed to clear the pressure in his buzzing ears. At least, he thought thankfully, the shaft was not closed at the top. They were not being borne upward to be crushed against an unyielding surface overhead.

Twice they flashed by other landing places abutting the shaft. After they passed the second Kartr squeezed his eyes shut. The sensation of being on a sideless elevator moving at some speed was one he believed he would never choose to experience again. It was infinitely worse—though akin to—the one attack of space fear he had had when he lost his mooring rope and had floated away from the ship while making repairs on the hull during flight.

"We're here—"

Kartr opened his eyes, very glad to hear a quaver in Rolth's voice. So the Faltharian had not enjoyed the voyage any more than he had!

Where was "here"? The sergeant scrambled off the plate, almost on all fours, and looked around him. The room in which they appeared was well lighted. Above him, rising to a dizzy height, reached floor after floor, all with galleries ringing upon the center. But he did not have long to examine that for a cry from Rolth brought him around.

"It's—it's gone!" The Faltharian was staring with wide eyes at the floor.

And he was entirely right. The plate-elevator on which they had just made that too swift ascent had vanished and the floor where it had entered was, as far as Kartr could see, now a smooth, unbroken stretch of pavement.

"It sank back"—Rolth's voice was under better control now—"and then a block came out from one side and sealed it."

"Which may account for the under ways not being discovered," suggested Kartr. "Suppose this shaft only opened when our car pulled up at the platform in the tunnel, or, because we started some other automatic control—it may be set to operate in that fashion—"

"I," Rolth stated firmly, "am going to stay away from the middle of rooms in here until we leave this blasted place. What if you were on the trapdoor and somebody stepped on the proper spot below? Regular trap!" He scowled at the floor and walked carefully, testing each step, to the nearest of the doorways. Kartr was almost inclined to follow his example. As the Faltharian had pointed out there was no way of knowing what other machinery their mere presence in the ancient buildings might activate. And then he wondered if it had been their sled's landing which had set the patroller to its work and so brought the robot upon them.

But a potential menace greater than machines which might or might not exist alerted him a few seconds later. There was an unknown and living creature ahead. The Arcturian? No. The strange mind he touched was not that strong. Whoever was before them now lacked the perception sense. Kartr need not fear betrayal until they were actually seen. Rolth caught the signal he made. And, while the Faltharian did not draw his blaster, his hand hovered just above its grip.

But the hall beyond the first door was empty. It was square and furnished with benches of an opaline substance. Under the subdued lighting, which came out of the walls themselves, sparks of rich color caught fire in the milky surface of the simply wrought pieces. This must be an ante-room of some sort. For in the opposite wall were set a pair of doors, twice Kartr's height, bearing the first relief sculpture he had seen in the city—conventionalized and symbolic representation of leaves. It was behind those doors that the other awaited them.

The sergeant began the tedious task of blocking out his own impressions, of concentrating only on that spark of life force hidden ahead. He was lucky in that the unknown was not a sensitive, that he could contact, could insert the mind touch, without betraying his own identity.

Human, yes. A point three and a half—no more. A point four would have been dimly aware of his spying—uneasy under it—a point five would have sensed him at once. But all this stranger knew was a discouragement, a mental fatigue. And—he was no pirate—or a prisoner of pirates—all feeling of violence past or present was lacking.

But—Kartr had already set his hand on the wide fastening of the door. Someone else had just joined the man in there. And from a first tentative contact the sergeant recoiled instantly. The Arcturian! In the same second he identified that mind, he knew that all hope of concealment was now over—that the Arcturian knew where they were as well as if his eyes could pierce stone and metal to see them. It was, Kartr's lip caught between his teeth, almost as if the Arcturian had dropped his own mind shield to bait them into showing themselves. And if that were so—! The ranger's green eyes were centered with a spark of dangerous yellow fire. He made a sign to Rolth.

Reluctantly the other's hand moved away from his blaster. Kartr studied him almost critically and then glanced down along the length of his own body. Their vlis hide boots and belts had survived without a scratch in spite of the rough life in the bush. And those blazing Comet badges were still gleaming on breast and helmet. Even if that Comet was modified by the crossed dart and leaf of a ranger it was the insignia of the Patrol. And he who wore it had authority to appear anywhere in the galaxy without question—in fact by rights the questions were his to ask.

Kartr bore down on the fastening of the doors. They came apart in the center, withdrawing in halves into the walls, leaving an opening wide enough for six men instead of just the two standing in it.

Here the light radiating from the walls was brighter and much of it was focused on an oval table in the exact center of the room—a table so long that the entire crew of a cruiser might have been accommodated around it. It was of the opaline stone and there were benches curved to follow its line.

Two men sat there, quietly enough, though, Kartr noted, a blaster lay close to the hand of the taller one— the Arcturian. But when *he* saw the badge of the Patrol his face was a mirror of amazement and he was on his feet in one swift movement. His slighter companion stared, licked his lips—and Kartr knew when his utter surprise turned into incredulous joy.

"The Patrol!" That was the Arcturian and there was

certainly no pleasure to be read in his identifying exclamation. But his mind block was tightly in place and Kartr could not know what lay behind those black, hooded eyes.

They were not pirates—those two. Both were dressed in the fantastically cut and colored tunics favored by the civilians of the decadent inner systems. And the blaster on the table was apparently their only weapon. Kartr strode forward.

"You are?" he demanded crisply, molding his stance and voice on Jaksan's. He had never before assumed the duties of a Patrolman, but as long as he wore the Comet no civilian would be allowed to guess that.

"Joyd Cummi, Vice-Sector Lord of Arcturus," the tall man answered almost sneeringly. He had the usual overbearing arrogance of his race. "This is my secretary, Fortus Kan. We were passengers on the Capella *X451*. She was attacked by pirates and went into over drive when in a damaged condition. When we came out we discovered that her computer had failed and we were in a totally unfamiliar section of the galaxy. We had fuel enough to cruise for two weeks and then it gave out and we were forced to land near here. We have been trying to communicate with some point of civilization but we had no idea that we were so successful! You are from—?"

A Vice-Sector Lord, eh? And an Arcturian into the bargain. Kartr was treading on dangerous ground now. But, he decided, he was not going to let this Joyd Cummi know that the Patrol had not arrived to rescue castaways—but as fellow refugees. There was a suggestion of something wrong here. His perception was alert, trying to measure words where he could not tap minds.

"We are Ranger Rolth and Ranger Sergeant Kartr, attached to the *Starfire*. We shall report your presence here to our commander."

"Then you did not come in answer to our signals?"

burst out Fortus Kan. His round boyish face was the acme of disappointment.

"We are engaged in a routine scouting mission," returned Kartr as coldly as he dared. The uneasiness in the atmosphere was growing stronger every moment. The Arcturian's shield might be strong but he could not altogether control all emotions. And he might not be trying to.

An Arcturian was a five point nine on the sensitive scale, yes. But unless Cummi had met one of Kartr's little-known race before—which was hardly likely since so few of them had ever volunteered for off-planet duty— he could not guess he was now facing a six point six!

"Then—" Fortus Kan's voice became close to a wail. "You can't get us away from here. But at least you can bring help—"

Kartr shook his head. "I will report your presence to my commanding officer. How many of you are here?"

"One hundred and fifty passengers and twenty-five crew members," Joyd Cummi returned crisply. "May I ask how you reached this building without our notice? We activated for our protection the patrol robots we found here—"

He was interrupted, much to his evident annoyance by Fortus Kan.

"Did you destroy that patroller?" he demanded eagerly. "The one on Cummi Way?"

Cummi Way! Kartr caught the significance of that. So the Vice-Sector Lord ruled here—enough to give his name arbitrarily to the main thoroughfare of the city.

"We deactivated a robot in what we thought a deserted city," he returned. "Since your being here is of importance we shall end our exploration and return immediately to our camp."

"Of course." Cummi was now the efficient executive. "We have been able to restore to running order several of the ground transportation vehicles we discovered here. Let one of them drive you back—"

"We flew in," Kartr countered swiftly. "And we shall return the same way. Long life, Vice-Sector Lord!" He raised his hand in the conventional salute. But he wasn't to escape so easily.

"At least you can be driven to where you left your flyer, Ranger Sergeant. There are other robot patrollers in use and it will be safer if one who knows their code accompanies you. We cannot afford to risk you of the Patrol—"

Kartr dared not refuse what so smoothly appeared to be a sensible suggestion. Yet—he knew that there was trouble here. He felt along his spine the cold prickle of fear which had warned him so many times in his life before. If he could only probe Fortus Kan! But he dared not try it when the Arcturian was there.

"I think it is best not to over-excite our people with the report of your arrival at just this moment," the Lord continued as he escorted the rangers back across the ante-room. "It will, of course, be encouraging for them to know that we have been contacted by the Patrol. Especially when, after five months of broadcasting from here on a feeble com, we had begun to believe that we were exiled for life. But I would prefer to discuss matters with your commander before allowing their hopes to arise. You probably noted Kan's response to your appearance. He saw in it the promise of an immediate return to the comforts of civilization. And since a Patrol ship could not possibly transport all of us we must make other arrangements—"

Twice during that speech the Arcturian had made assaults at Kartr's mind, trying to learn—or—trying to win control? But the sergeant had his shield up and he knew that Cummi would only receive carefully planted impressions of a Patrol ship set down in a far district, a ship under the command of an alert and forceful officer, a difficult man for a civilian administrator to overawe.

"I think you are wise, Vice-Sector Lord," Kartr inserted into the first oral pause. "You have been here for five months then—within this city?"

"Not at first, no. We made an emergency landing some miles from here. But the city had registered on our photoscreens when we came down and we were able to locate it without undue difficulty. Its functions are in an amazing state of preservation—we must consider that we have been unusually favored by fortune. Of course, having Trestor Vink and two of his assistants among our number was an additional aid. He is the mech-techneer for the Capella line. And he has become quite absorbed in the mechanics here. He believes that originally its inhabitants were in some ways more advanced than we are. Yes, we have been very lucky."

They crossed the room of the hidden elevator shaft and came out on a vast balcony overhanging a hall so large that Kartr felt swallowed up in space. There was a stairway from the balcony to the lower floor of the hall—a flight of steps so wide that it might have been fashioned to accommodate a race of giants. And the lower hall opened through a series of tree-like pillars into the street.

"Coombs!"

The figure lounging against one of the pillars snapped to attention.

"You will take the road vehicle and drive these Patrolmen to their ship. I do not say good-bye, Sergeant." The Lord turned to Kartr with the graciousness of a great man addressing an admitted inferior. "We shall meet again soon. You have done a very good night's work and we are exceedingly grateful to you. Please inform your commanding officer that we shall be eagerly waiting to hear from him."

Kartr saluted. At least the Arcturian was not insisting

upon going with them to the sled. But he did stand there until they had taken their places in the small car and the driver put it into motion.

As they moved away from the building Kartr turned his attention to the driver. That bristling shock of black hair with its odd brindling of brown showed up clearly as they swept beneath one of the banners of city light—the long jaws, too. So—that was why Cummi let them go off alone! No wonder he had not thought it necessary to accompany them himself. He would be with them in one way if not bodily. Their driver was a Can-hound, the perfect servant whose mind was only a receiving set used for the benefit of his master.

Kartr's skin roughened as if something slimy trailed across him. He had the sensitive's inborn horror for the creature before him—a thing he would not dignify as either human or Bemmy. And now he would have to—have to—! The very thought made him so sick that his empty stomach twisted. This was the worst, the lowest task he had ever had forced upon him. He would have to go into that mind, skillfully enough not to be detected by the distant master, and there implant some false memories—

"Which way?" Even that voice rasped sickeningly along his nerves.

"Along this wide street here," he ordered with stiff lips. His hand closed over Rolth's. The Faltharian did not move but he answered with a light return pressure.

Kartr began, while his mouth twisted into a tortured ring of disgust and his mind and body alike fought wildly against the will which forced him to do this thing. It was worse than he had expected, he was degraded, soiled unspeakably by that contact. But he went on. Suddenly the car pulled to the side of the street, wavered into an open space between buildings, came to a stop in a courtyard. They remained in it while Kartr fought the miserable battle to the end. That came when the Can-hound's head fell forward and he slumped limply in the driver's seat.

Rolth got out. But Kartr had to steady himself with his hands as he followed. He reeled across the court and hung retching on a window sill. Then Rolth reached him and steadied his shaking body. With the Faltharian's arm still around him, the sergeant wavered out on the street.

"Just ahead—" Kartr got out the words painfully between spasms of sickness.

"Yes, I have seen."

The faint gleam of radiation was undoubtedly clearer to Rolth's light-sensitive eyes than it was to his own. They were about four blocks now from the point where the robot had fired at the doorway. And from there they could easily find their marked trail back to the sled.

Rolth asked no questions. He was there, a hand ready to support, a vast comforting glow of clean friendship. Clean—! Kartr wondered if he would ever feel clean again. How could a sensitive—even an Arcturian—deal with and through a creature such as that? But he mustn't think of the Can-hound now.

He was walking steadily again by the time they detoured around the atomic fire in the doorway. And he turned the walk into a ground-covering lope as the Faltharian retraced the trail he had earlier marked. When they got to the sled Kartr made a single suggestion.

"Lay a crossed course out of here—they may have some sort of scanner on us—"

Rolth grunted an assent. The sled took to the air. A cold wind, heralding the dawn, cut into them. Kartr wanted to wash in it, wash away the filth of the encounter with the Can-hound.

"You do not want them to know about us?" That was half question, half statement.

"It isn't up to me—that's Jaksan's problem," returned Kartr, out of a vast and overwhelming weariness. The

84

drain of that mind battle had almost meant a drain of life force too. He wanted to lie down and sleep, just sleep. But he couldn't. And he forced himself to give Rolth an explanation of what they had been pitted against—what they might have to fear in the future.

"That driver was a Can-hound. And there is something very wrong—completely wrong back there."

Rolth might not be a sensitive but as a ranger he knew a lot. He snapped out a biting word or two in his own tongue.

"I had to get into his mind—to make him a set of false memories. He will report back that he took us to the sled, certain things we were supposed to have said during the trip—the direction in which we departed—"

"So that was what you were doing!" Rolth's dark eyes lifted from the course indicator long enough to favor his companion with a look in which respect and awe were mingled.

Kartr relaxed, his head drooped to rest on the back of the seat. Now that they were out of the glare of the city the stars shone palely overhead. How as Jaksan going to handle this? Would he order them in to unite with the castaways in the city? If so—what about Cummi? What was he doing—planning right now?

"You distrust the Arcturian?" Rolth demanded as they streaked north on the evasive path Kartr had suggested.

"He is an Arcturian—you know them. He is a Vice-Sector Lord, there is no doubt he is in complete command in the city. And—he would not take kindly to having his rule disputed—"

"So he might not be in favor of the Patrol?"

"Maybe. Sector Lords are uneasy enough nowadays—there is a pull and tug of power. I would like very much to know why he was making a trip on an ordinary passenger ship anyway. If he—"

"Were getting away from some local hot spot he would

be only too glad to found a new kingdom here? Yes, that I can well understand," said Rolth. "Now we go home—"

The sled made a long curve to the right. Rolth shut off the propulsion rockets, kept on only the hover screens. They drifted slowly on the new course. It would take time, add an extra hour or so to their return journey. But unless the city had something new in scanners they were now off every spy screen.

They did very little talking for the rest of the trip. Kartr dozed off once and awoke with a start from a black dream. The need for complete rest drugged his mind when he tried to flog his weary brain into making plans. He would report the situation to Jaksan. The arms officer was hostile to the impressions of a sensitive—he might not welcome Kartr's description of the unease in the city. And the sergeant had no proof to back his belief that the farther they stayed away from Cummi the better. Why did he fear Cummi? Was it because he was an Arcturian, another sensitive? Or was it because of the Can-hound? Why was he so sure that the Vice-Sector Lord was a dangerous enemy?

7

## *THE RANGERS*
## *STAND TOGETHER*

"You must admit that his account was plausible enough—"

Kartr faced Jaksan across the flat rock which served the camp as a table.

"And the city," persisted the arms officer mercilessly, "is in an excellent state of preservation. Not only that, but this party from the *X451* includes mech-techneers who have been able to start it functioning again—"

The sergeant nodded wearily. He should have brought to this contest of will a clear mind and a rested body. Instead he ached with both mental and physical fatigue. It was an effort to hold his stand against the hammering disapproval of the other.

"If all this *is* true"—Jaksan reached what he certainly believed to be a logical and sensible conclusion—for the third time—"I cannot understand this reluctance of yours, Kartr. Unless—" he was radiating hostility again but the sergeant was almost too tired to care—"unless you have taken a dislike to this Arcturian for personal reasons." Then he paused and his hostility was broken for an instant by an emotion close to sympathy. "Wasn't it an Arcturian who gave the order to burn off Ylene?"

"It might have been for all I know. But that is not the

87

reason why I distrust this Joyd Cummi," began Kartr with such remnants of patience as he could muster.

There was no use in making an issue of Cummi's use of the Can-hound. Only another sensitive could understand the true horror of that. Jaksan had settled on an explanation for Kartr's attitude which was reasonable to him and he would hold to it. The sergeant had learned long ago that those who were not sensitives had a deep distrust of perception and the mind touch and some refused to even admit its existence as a fact. Jaksan was almost of that group—he would believe in Kartr's ability to meet and deal with animals and strange non-humans, but he inwardly repudiated the sergeant's being able to contact or read his fellow men. There was no arguing with him on that point. Kartr sighed. He had done what he could to prevent what he knew would be Jaksan's next move. Now he could only wait for the menace he believed was in the city to show itself.

So they made the journey to join the *X451's* survivors, and they admitted, against all Kartr's pleas, their own shipwrecked condition. Joyd Cummi greeted them with urbane and welcoming ease. There was a ship's medico to attend to Vibor—there were luxurious quarters in, as Kartr noted with suspicion, corridors adjacent to the Vice-Sector Lord's own, for the crewmen and the officers.

The welcome granted the rangers was, however, somewhat cooler. Kartr and Rolth were accepted, given subtly to understand that, as humans, they would stand equal with the commoners of Cummi's kingdom. But the Arcturian had given Zinga and Fylh no more than a nod and made no suggestions for their lodging. Kartr gathered his small command together in the center of a large bare room where no eavesdropper could possibly listen in.

"If," Zinga said as they settled themselves cross-legged on the floor, "you still maintain that the odor issuing through these halls is far from flower-like, I shall agree with you! How long"—he turned to Kartr—"are you going to let some ragged tails of loyalty pull you into situations such as this?"

Fylh's claws rasped along the hard scales on the other's forearm.

"Rangers should only speak when spoken to. And Bemmy rangers must let their superiors decide what is best for them. Such must be dutiful and humble and keep their places—"

The close guard which Kartr had kept upon his temper ever since his warning had been so quickly disregarded and they had come to this place which appeared to him to be a trap was burned away by that.

"I've heard enough of that!"

"Zinga has a point," Rolth paid no attention to Kartr's outbreak. "We either accept the prevailing conditions here—or we leave—if we can. And maybe we can't wait too long or be half way about it."

" 'If we can,' " repeated Zinga with a grin displaying no humor but many sharp teeth. "That is a most interesting suggestion, Rolth. I wonder if there were—or are—any Bemmys numbered in the crew or among the passengers of the *X451*. You notice that I am inclined to use the past tense when I refer to them. Indications would make that seem proper."

Kartr studied his two brown hands, one protruding from the dirty sling, the other resting on his knee. They were scratched and calloused, the nails worn down. But though he was examining each one of those scratches with minute attention he was really absorbed in the nasty implications of Zinga's words. No—he didn't have to accept matters as they were. He should make a few preparations of his own.

"Where are our packs?" he asked Zinga.

Both eyelids clicked in a slow wink. "Those creatures

are under our eye. If we have to leave in a hurry we'll be able to do so with full tramping equipment."

"I shall suggest to Jaksan that the rangers take quarters on their own—together—" Kartr said slowly.

"There is a three-story tower on the west corner of this building," cut in Fylh. "Should we withdraw to that lofty perch—well, it may be that they will be so glad to be rid of us that they will permit it."

"Let ourselves be bottled up?" asked Zinga with some sting in his hissing voice.

Fylh clicked his claws with an irritated snap. "No one is going to be bottled up. Please remember we are dealing with highly civilized city dwellers, not explorers. To them all possible passages in and out of a building are accounted for by windows and doors only."

"Then this tower of yours boasts some feature not included in that catalogue which would serve us in a pinch?" There was a little smile curving Rolth's pale lips.

"Naturally. Or I would not have seen its possibilities as our stronghold. There are a series of bands projecting in a pattern down the outer walls. As good as a staircase to someone who knows how to use fingers and toes—"

"And keep his eyes closed while he does it," groaned Zinga. "Sometimes I wish *I* were civilized and could lead a sane and peaceful life."

"We could allow"—Fylh had talked himself back into his best humor again—"these people to believe that we are safely out of mischief. They can put a guard at the single stairway leading up in that tower if they wish."

Kartr nodded. "I'll see Jaksan. After all, we may be rangers, but we are also Patrol. And if we want to stick together no civilian has any right to question us—Vice-Sector Lord or not! Stay out of trouble now."

He got up and the three nodded. They might not be sensitives—though he suspected that Zinga had some power akin to his, but they knew that they were only four in a potentially dangerous environment. If they could just get themselves exiled into Fylh's tower!

But he had to wait a long time to see Jaksan. The arms officer had accompanied Vibor to the medico. And when he at last returned to his quarters and found Kartr waiting for him, he was anything but cordial.

"What do you want now? The Vice-Sector Lord has been asking for you. He had some orders—"

"Since when," Kartr interrupted, "has even a Vice-Sector Lord had orders for one of the Patrol? He may advise and request—he does not order any wearer of the Comet, patrolman or ranger!"

Jaksan had crossed to the window and now he stood there, tapping his nails against the casing, his shoulders and back stubbornly presented to the sergeant. He did not turn when he answered:

"I do not believe that you take our position now into proper consideration, Sergeant. We do not have a ship. We—"

"And since when has a ship been necessary?" But maybe that was the exact truth, right there. Maybe to Jaksan and the crew the ship *was* necessary—without it they were naked, at a loss. "It is because I feared this very thing," he continued more quietly, "that I was against our coming here." Whether it was politic or not he had to say that.

"Under the circumstances we had very little choice in the matter!" Jaksan showed some of his old fire in that burst. "Great Space, man, would you have us fight the wilderness for food and shelter when there was this to come to? What of the Commander? He had to have medical attention. Only a—" He stopped in mid-sentence.

"Why not finish that, sir? Only a barbarian ranger would argue against it. Is that what you want to say? Well, I maintain, barbarian that I am, that it is better to be free in the wilderness than to come here. But let me have this

91

clear—am I to understand that you have surrendered the authority of the Patrol to Joyd Cummi?"

"Divided authority is bad." But Jaksan refused to turn and face him. "It is necessary that each man contribute his skills to help the community. Joyd Cummi has discovered evidence that there is a severe cold season coming. It is our duty to help prepare for that. I think he wishes to send out hunting parties as food may be a problem. There are women and children to provide for—"

"I see. And the rangers are to take over the hunting? Well, we shall make a few plans. In the meantime we will take quarters for ourselves. And it might be well to arrange those with an eye to the future—unless there is also a butcher to be found among these city men."

"You and Rolth were assigned rooms here—"

"The rangers prefer to remain as a unit. As you know, that is only Patrol policy. Or has the Patrol totally ceased to exist?" If Kartr had not been needled by increasing uneasiness he might not have added that.

"See here, Kartr." Jaksan turned away from the window. "Isn't it about time that you looked straight at some hard facts? We're going to be here for the rest of our lives. We are seven men against almost two hundred—and they have a well-organized community going—"

"Seven men?" queried Kartr. "We number nine if you count the Commander."

"Men." Jaksan stressed the word.

There it was—out in the open. Kartr had feared to hear it for a long time now.

"There are four qualified Patrol rangers and five of you," he returned stubbornly. "And the rangers stick together."

"Don't be a fool!"

"Why shouldn't I have that privilege?" Kartr's rage was ice cold now. "All the rest of you seem to enjoy it."

"You're a human being! You belong with your kind. These aliens—they—"

"Jaksan"—Kartr repudiated once and for all the leadership of the arms officer—"I know all those threadbare, stock arguments. There is no need to run through them again. I have had them dinned into me by your kind ever since I joined the Service and asked for ranger detail—"

"You young idiot! Since you joined the Service, eh? And how long ago was that? Eight years? Ten? You're no more than a cub now. Since you joined the Service! You don't know anything at all about it—this Bemmy problem. Only a barbarian—"

"We'll admit that I'm a barbarian and that I have queer tastes in friends, shall we? Admit it and leave it out of this conversation!" Kartr was gaining control of his temper.

It was plain that Jaksan was attempting to justify some stand he had taken or been forced into agreement with, not only to Kartr but to himself.

"Suppose you allow me to go to perdition my own way. Is this 'All humans stand together' a rule of Cummi's?"

Jaksan refused to meet the sergeant's demanding gaze. "He is very prejudiced. Don't forget he is an Arcturian. They had an internal problem in that system when they had to deal with a race of alien non-humans—"

"And they solved that problem neatly and expediently by the cold-blooded massacre of the aliens!"

"I forgot—your feeling against Arcturians—"

"My feeling for Arcturians, which, I might say, is different from the one you deem it to be, has nothing to do with this case. I simply refuse now or ever to hold any such views against any stranger, human or Bemmy. If the Vice-Sector Lord wants the rangers to do his hunting—all right. But we shall stick together as a unit. And if to continue to do so means trouble—then we might oblige in that direction also!"

"Look here." Jaksan kicked moodily at the bedroll which lay on the floor. "Don't stop thinking about it, Kartr. We'll have to live the rest of our lives here. We're really lucky beyond our dreams—Cummi believes that this city can be almost entirely restored. We can start all over. I know that you don't care for Cummi, but he is able enough to organize a shipload of hysterical passengers into a going settlement. Seven men can't fight him. All I ask of you for the present is don't repeat to Cummi what you just said to me. Think it over first."

"I shall. In the meantime the rangers will take quarters together."

"Oh, all right." Jaksan shrugged. "Do it—wherever you please."

"Maybe he should have said where Cummi pleases," thought Kartr as he left the room.

He found the rangers waiting for him and gave his own orders.

"Rolth, you and Fylh get up to that tower. If anyone tries to stop you pull Patrol rank on him. It may still carry some weight with the underlings here. Zinga, where did you leave our packs?"

Five minutes later Kartr and the Zacathan gathered the four pioneer packs. "Slip an anti-gravity disc under them," said Kartr, "and come on."

With the packs floating just off the floor and easy to tow, they made their way toward the rear of the building. But, as they approached the narrow flight of stairs Zinga said led to the roof, they were met by Fortus Kan. He edged back against the wall to let them pass, since Kartr did not halt. But he asked as they went by:

"Where are you going?"

"Settling in ranger quarters," the sergeant returned briefly.

"That one is still watching us," Zinga whispered as they

mounted. "He is none too stout of heart. A good loud shout of wrath aimed at him would send him scuttling—"

"But don't try it," Kartr returned. "There is enough trouble before us now without stirring up any more."

"Ho! So you learned that, did you? Well, a short life and a merry one, as my egg brother often said while we were still shipmates. I wonder where Ziff is now—rolling in silk and eating brofids three times a day if I know that black-hearted despoiler! Not that it wouldn't be good to see his ugly face awaiting us above when we have finished this climb. His infighting is excellent, a very handy man with a force blade. Zippp—and there's an enemy down with half his insides gone—"

They could do, thought Kartr bitterly, with about fifty good infighters right now—or even with only ten.

"Welcome home, travelers!" That was Rolth, his goggled eyes lending his face an insect-like outline as he looked down at them. "For once the old pepper bird has found us a real perch. Come in and relax, my brave boys!"

"Flame bats and Octopods!" Even Zinga seemed truly amazed as he stared about the room they entered.

The walls were a murky translucent green. And behind them came and went shapes of vivid color, water creatures swimming! Then Kartr saw that it was an illusion born of light and some sort of automatic picture projection. Zinga sat down on the packs, bearing them under his weight to the floor.

"Luscious! Luscious! Enough to tempt the most fastidious palate. The being who planned this room was a gourmand. I would be proud to shake his hand, fin or tentacle. Magnificent! That red one—does it not resemble almost to the last scale the succulent brofid? What a wonderful, wonderful room!"

"What about rations?" Kartr inquired of Rolth over Zinga's head.

The Faltharian's eyebrows raised until they could be seen over the rim of his goggles. "Are you contemplating our sitting out a siege? We have a few basic supply tins still unopened—about five days of full meals—twice that if we have to draw in our belts."

"Do you mean to tell me," Zinga broke out, "that you have brought me into this place of culinary promise and now propose to feed me extract of nourishing—bah—what a word, nourishing! As if nourishment and *food* are ever the same—to feed me extract of fungus and the rest of that non-exciting goo we have to absorb when we are climbing over bare rock with no chance of hunting! This is a torture which cannot be refined upon. I insist upon my rights as a freeborn citizen—"

"A freeborn citizen?" queried Fylh. "Second class—third class twice removed, would be much more apt. And you have no rights at all—"

But Rolth had been watching Kartr's expression and now he broke in.

"Is that the way of it—honestly?"

"Just about, I'm afraid." Kartr sat down on the room's single piece of furniture—an opaline bench. "I went to Jaksan. He said Cummi had orders for me—"

"Orders?" Again the Faltharian's eyebrows betrayed his surprise. "A civilian giving orders to the Patrol? We may be rangers, but we are also still Patrol!"

"Are we?" Fylh wondered. "A Patrolman has ships, force to back him up. We're just survivors now, and we can't ring in the fleet if we get in a tight place—"

"Jaksan agrees with that. I gathered that he has more or less abdicated in Cummi's favor. The idea is that the Vice-Sector Lord has a running concern here—"

"And that we are more or less lucky to be included in?" demanded Rolth. "Yes, I can see that argument being advanced. But Jaksan—he's veteran Patrol to the core. Somehow his standing aside this way—it doesn't fit!"

Fylh made a gesture of brushing aside nonessentials. "Jaksan's psychological response need not concern us as much as something else. Do I gather that here Bemmys *are* second class citizens?"

"Yes." That answer was bald but Kartr saw no need to temper it.

"I take it that you were urged to—er—withdraw from contagion," Zinga drawled, leaning back and hooking his taloned fingers over his knees.

"That was part of it."

"How stupid can they get?" Rolth wanted to know. "If they want us to do their hunting, they must need food. And a bunch of these soft inner system men are not going to get much game by running out and beating the bushes. Instead of antagonizing us they ought to be making concessions."

"When did you ever know prejudice to act logically? And Jaksan seems to have agreed to this down-with-the-Bemmys plan, hasn't he?" Fylh's red eyes had gleams in them not very pleasant to see.

"I don't know what's happened to Jaksan," Kartr exploded. "And I don't care! It's what is going to happen to us which is more important right now—"

"You and Rolth," Fylh pointed out, "need not worry—"

Kartr jumped to his feet and took two strides across the room so that his green eyes were on a level and boring into those round red ones.

"That is the last time I ever want to hear anything like that! I told Jaksan and I shall tell Cummi—if it becomes necessary—that the rangers stand together."

Fylh's thin lips shut. Then the hard points of fire in his eyes softened. He made a small soothing gesture with his claws and when he spoke his voice was even again.

"What was Jaksan's reaction to your speech?"

"Just a lot of words. But it gave me an excellent chance of putting through our coming here together."

Zinga had arisen and was prowling around the room. "Done any more exploring, you two?" he asked Rolth. "What's the layout?"

"One more room beyond that archway on this floor. It has two windows both of which overhang Fylh's outside stairway. There is one large room immediately above this one and a third over that with a bathroom off. Believe it or not—the water is running in that!"

Kartr disregarded Zinga's exclamation of approval. "Only the one way in—unless someone climbs up the wall? Sure of that?"

"Yes. Of course they might descend upon us from the sky. But I hardly think we need fear that. And this door can be locked—watch—"

Rolth trod on a dull red block set in the floor. A door moved silently out of the right wall and sealed the entrance. On it was a metal plate and the Faltharian set his hand on it for an instant.

"Now try to get that open," he urged the sergeant.

But, even when Zinga and Fylh added their strength to his, Kartr was unable to force the door. Then Rolth stepped again on the stone and it opened easily.

"Fylh locked me out when we were exploring and we had a time finding out how to open it again. Tricky, the fellows who built that—even if they were so primitive as to use atomics. It would take a full size disruptor to breach that."

"Which leads me to wonder if they do have one of those." Zinga put Kartr's thought into words.

But then that worry was blocked out for he sensed someone coming up the stairs. At the sergeant's signal the rangers melted away. Zinga was now flat against the wall beside the door where he could be at the back of anyone

98

who entered before the stranger would know of his presence. Fylh lay belly down behind the pile of packs, and Rolth had drawn his blaster, standing a little behind the sergeant who waited, his good hand empty.

"Kartr!"

They knew the voice but they did not relax.

"Come in."

Smitt obeyed. He gave a start as Zinga materialized behind him. But there was a worried frown on his face and Kartr knew that he was no danger to them. For the second time the com-techneer had come to them because he was in trouble and not because he was an enemy.

"What is it?" asked the sergeant with very little welcome. After all Smitt was to be normally reckoned with Jaksan's forces.

"They're talking—a lot. They've said you rangers are too alien to be trusted."

"Well"—Kartr's lips curled back in what was not even a shadow of a smile—"I've heard that a good many times before and I can't see that we're any the worse for it."

"Maybe you weren't—before. But this Arcturian—he's—the man must be mad!" Smitt exploded. "I tell you"—his voice slid up the scale a little—"he must be raving mad!"

"Suppose," hissed Zinga, "you just sit down—over there where we can keep an eye on you—and tell us all about it."

# 8

## *PALACE REVOLUTION*

"That's it— I've practically nothing concrete to tell. It's just a kind of feeling—the way he persists in keeping us away from all but his own men. He has a guard—that Can-hound, a couple of jetmen from the *X451*, one of the officers, two intal planters, and three professional mercenaries. They're all armed—Control issue blasters and force blades. But I haven't heard of or seen any of the other officers from the *X451*. And Cummi's taken over—gives commands to *us!* Dalgre and Snyn were sent to join his techneers and help run the city. Ordered to do so, mind you—and they Patrolmen! And Jaksan didn't make any objection."

"And what about you—has he drafted you yet?" asked Rolth.

"Luckily I wasn't there when they came hunting techneer recruits. Look here—how does he dare give orders to the Patrol?" There was honest bewilderment in Smitt's voice.

For the second time Kartr explained. "Better get it into your head, Smitt, that as far as you, and Cummi, and the rest of us are concerned, the Patrol has ceased to exist.

We've nothing to back up any show of authority—he has. That is just why—"

"You argued against our coming here?" Smitt's lips thinned. Kartr felt the other's rage. "Well, you were right! I know you rangers don't feel the same about the Service as we crewmen do. You've always been independent cusses. But my father died on the barricades at the Altra air locks—one of the rear guard who held their posts long enough for the survivors' ships to leave. And my grandfather was second officer of the Promixa dreadnaught when she tried to make the Second Galaxy. We've served five generations in the Patrol. And may I be Space-burned if I ever take orders from a Cummi while I still wear this!" His hand went to his Comet badge.

"A very fine sentiment which will not help you any if Cummi's private police force come a-hunting," Zinga remarked. "But was it just this disinclination to take orders from a mere civilian which drove you to us?"

"You," Smitt snapped at the Zacathan, "needn't be so cocky. I overheard enough to learn that Cummi is death on fraternization with Bemmys and that goes for rangers, too," he aimed in Kartr's direction. "There's a rumor, it came in the form of a secondhand warning from one of the intal planters, that Cummi's had a couple burned already—"

"A couple of what?" That was Fylh, and his crest was rising. "Bemmys? Of what species?"

Smitt shook his head. "I don't know, the planter was vague. Only, you're not going to get a fair deal from Cummi, that's plain. And I'm not going to take his orders. Maybe we haven't always spaced the same course before, but we have a common problem before us now."

"So?" Fylh's claws preened his crest. "But the best of the bargain seems to be yours under the circumstances. What do you have to offer us in return?"

"He has something we might need," Kartr broke in.

The appeal of the com-techneer was an honest one. He did want to throw in with them.

"It will depend upon you, Smitt. Can you swallow your pride enough to co-operate with Cummi's party—co-operate until you can learn something of their set-up—how much power Cummi really has, whether there are any rebels among the passengers, what are some of his future plans? We're not"—he spoke now to the rangers—"going to strike out blindly. You two, Fylh and Zinga, will have to lie low until we do know how we stand. No use attracting any attention. As for me, since my talk with Jaksan, I am doubtless down in their black books with a double star. Rolth is handicapped for daytime work. So, Smitt, if you are really willing to join up with us, keep that wish under mind block—and I mean *under* block. The Arcturian is a sensitive and what he can't scrape out of an unsuspecting mind the Can-hound may be able to get for him. It'll be a tough assignment, Smitt. You've got to join the anti-Bemmy, pro-Cummi crowd—at least with luke-warm attachment. A little initial rebellion is all right, they would expect that from a Patrolman with your background. But can you play a double game, Smitt—and do you want to?"

The com-techneer had listened quietly and now he raised his head and nodded.

"I can try. I don't know about this mind block business." He hesitated. "I'm no sensitive. How much can Cummi do with me?"

"He's a five point nine. He can't take you over, if that is what you're afraid of. You're from Luga—or your family was Lugan stock originally, weren't they?"

"My father was Lugan. My mother came from Desart."

"Lugan—Desart—" Kartr looked to Zinga.

"High resistance core," the Zacathan informed him promptly. "Imaginative, but excellent control. Perception zero-zero-eight. No, no Arcturian could take him over.

102

And you do have a mind block, Smitt, whether you've ever tried to use it or not. Just think about some com-machine when you're around a sensitive. Concentrate on some phase of your old job—"

"Like this?" demanded Smitt eagerly.

It was as if he had snapped off some switch. Where Smitt sat there was now a mental blank. Kartr bit off an exclamation and then said:

"Keep that up, Smitt! Zinga—!"

His own power went out toward the com-techneer, and then he felt a second stream of energy unite with it, driving into that blankness with him like the tip of a blaster beam. So, he had been right! Zinga was a sensitive, too, and to a degree he could not even measure. Together their wills smashed at Smitt, smashed on a barrier which held as staunchly as the hull of a space ship.

There were beads of moisture on Kartr's forehead, gathering under the edge of his helmet to trickle down his cheeks and chin. Then his free hand moved in a gesture of defeat and he relaxed.

"You need not worry about mind invasion, Smitt. Unless you get careless."

The com-techneer was on his feet. "Then we are allied?" He asked that almost shyly, as if he had come there expecting to be turned away.

"We are. Just stir around some and see what you can find out. But don't, if possible, get sent off from here where we can't reach you. We may have to move fast if trouble comes."

"I shan't—" Smitt crossed to the door. Now he hesitated and turned. And before he went out his hand moved in a gesture which included all of them—human and Bemmy alike—the full salute of a Patrolman to his equals.

"Now—just in case—" Fylh flitted across the room and

stamped on the door-controlling block, locking the portal with the heat of his claws.

"Yes," Zinga agreed, "one does feel more relaxed when it isn't necessary to think about guarding one's back. Shall we settle in?"

Kartr slipped his left wrist out of the sling and rubbed it thoughtfully.

"They have a medico here. I wonder——"

Rolth moved up beside him. "Are you thinking of venturing into the slith's cave alone?"

"A well-equipped ship's hospital should include a renewer ray. And I'd like to go into battle—if I have to—with two good hands instead of one. Also it gives me a legitimate excuse for wandering around below. I can ask questions——"

"All right. But you don't go alone," Rolth agreed. "Somehow I don't fancy any of us prancing about alone in this building. Two's pretty good company—and two blasters can clear a wider path than one."

"None of that! I'm a sufferer in search of a medico, remember?" But Kartr's lips stretched in what had come during these past days to be an unfamiliar curve, a genuine smile. "Have you two enough to amuse yourselves with while we are gone?"

"Don't worry about us." Zinga grinned and his inch fangs shone in the greenish light to ghoulish advantage. "We shall set up housekeeping. We do, I take it, lock the door behind you?"

"Yes. And you open it only when you pick up our mind patterns."

Zinga didn't even blink at that. Of course, he had revealed the extent of his power when he had aided Kartr in attacking Smitt's block. But, with his usual disregard for human emotions, he apparently saw no reason for discussing his long concealment now.

Fylh opened the door and they started down the stairs.

It was quiet below and they were almost into the corridor before Kartr's perception warned him of a stranger's approach. It was a young man, in the rather ornate uniform of a passenger ship's officer, who strode confidently toward them.

"You are Sergeant Kartr?"

"I am."

"The Vice-Sector Lord wishes to see you."

Kartr stopped and gazed with mild interest at the newcomer. Perhaps the sergeant was even a year or so younger than this assured Flight Spacer—allowing for planetary and racial difference—but suddenly he felt almost grandfatherly.

"I have not received any orders from my superior officer delegating me to be attached to the service of the Central Control Civil Section."

And for a wonder that pomposity actually disconcerted the other. Maybe the old magic of the Patrol still held a small power. Kartr and Rolth started on, passed the officer, and were several feet down the hall before he caught up with them again.

"See here!" He tried to project the sting of an order into his voice, but it faded when both rangers wheeled to give him grave and courteous attention. "The Lord Cummi—he is in charge here, you know," he ended lamely.

"Section six, paragraph eight, general orders," answered Rolth. " 'The Patrol is the guardian of the law under Central Control. It may assist the civil branch if and when requested to do so. But at no time and in no manner does it surrender its authority to any planetary or sectional advisor or ruler, except under the direct seal and order of Central Control.' "

The youngster stood with his mouth slightly open. The last thing he had expected, thought Kartr with a relieving chuckle of real humor which he was able to suppress, was to have general orders spouted in his face. Zinga would have loved to hear this. Kartr hoped that the Zacathan had followed them mentally and *was* enjoying it.

"But—" Whatever protest the Spacer was about to make died away as the rangers' expressions of polite but impatient attention did not alter.

"Now," Kartr said when the officer added nothing to that forlorn "but," "perhaps you can direct me to your medico's quarters. I require attention for this." He indicated his wrist.

The officer was eager to oblige. "Down two flights of stairs at the end of this corridor and turn to your right. Medico Tre has the first four rooms in that hall."

He remained where he was, still staring after them as they moved on.

"What do you suppose he is going to report to the great Cummi?" Rolth wondered as they followed directions. "I don't think that I would care to be in his boots. Do you believe—"

"That I was wise to stand up and resist at this point? Maybe I wasn't, but they must have discovered from Jaksan that I am hostile. And"—Kartr's face was entirely expressionless—"that was something I had to do. He set the Can-hound on us!"

And Rolth, having seen that fighting face before and knowing what its mask covered, decided to say no more.

They met no one else on those two flights of stairs. Apparently this portion of Cummi's stronghold was more or less deserted. And they were approaching the first door along the medico's corridor when a thin whisper of sound caught their attention. Here the tall windows were set in deep recesses and it was from one of those that the summons came.

"A woman—"

But Kartr already knew that, having met the block which always prevented a sensitive from interpreting the emotions of one of the opposite sex. She was leaning forward, daring to beckon with one hand. Rolth edged toward that side of the hall and Kartr nodded. The Faltharian would contact the woman while the sergeant kept on to their destination. If any one except Zinga had a mind watch on them at present such a move might be confusing.

Rolth stepped into the embrasure and drew back against the window, taking the woman with him. To anyone not directly before the recess they were not visible. Kartr went on a yard and glanced back. Rolth had made the right move—from where he was now they could not be seen.

The sergeant turned into the next open door. Medico's quarters all right from the equipment in sight. Almost at the same instant a tall man came from an inner room. Kartr tried mind contact and then lost some of his tension. This was no Arcturian, and no enemy either. He could scan nothing but good will in the other's mind.

"You have a renewer ray?" he asked, drawing his arm out of the sling.

"We have. How long it will continue to function locked to these city currents is another question. We cannot be sure of anything. I am Medico Lasilo Tre. A break?" His fingers were already busy about Kartr's wrist, unfastening the bandages Zinga had put on that morning.

"I don't know. Ah—" Kartr sucked in his breath as Tre began probing the bruised and purple flesh.

Then the ranger was pushed down on a stool at the edge of the renewer beam, his throbbing arm stretched out under the concentrated ray, feeling again the draw of those invisible healing motes. Twice Tre snapped off the current and came to examine the hurt with delicate finger tips—only to turn it on again after shaking his head. The third time he was satisfied. Kartr lifted his arm gingerly and flexed first his fingers and then his wrist. Although he had once before been under the ray—to renew a leg almost chewed to pieces—the wonder of the restoration was as great as ever. He pulled off his sling and grinned happily at the medico.

"Better than new," Tre commented. "Only wish that your officer could be as easily put to rights, Sergeant—"

Vibor! Kartr had almost forgotten the Commander. "How is he?"

Tre frowned. "The physical wounds—those we were able to heal. But the other— I'm no psycho-sensitive. He needs the type of care and treatment he'll never be able to get now—unless a miracle occurs and we are rescued—"

"Which you do not believe will ever happen," suggested Kartr.

"How can any sensible man believe that we will?" countered the medico. But there was something else, another emotion hidden beneath that answer. "This planet—this solar system—does not even exist on any map the *X451* carried."

"But those who built this city were at a high level of civilization," Kartr pointed out. "Where did they go?"

"They were and they weren't. Mechanically they were far advanced, yes. But there are odd gaps. I understand you rangers are trained to assess strange civilizations. I shall be eager to have your reaction to the ruins of this one after you have had the time to study it. The one thing I *have* noticed is that there is no space port here and there never was. Maybe the men of this world never knew space flight—"

"But what happened to them?"

Tre shrugged. "At least this is no second Tantor. We made sure of that before we entered the city. And we have found no human remains here. It seems almost as if they all walked away one day, leaving their city ready and waiting, all geared to go again when they wished to return. There are signs of time—some erosion. The machinery, though, had all been left protected, oiled, laid up in such a way as to set our mech-techneers running around begging people to come and look at an excellent preservation job."

"They must have planned on returning, then." Kartr digested that. Was there, on some other land mass of this unknown world, a remnant of civilization?

"If they did they were prevented. It has been a long time since they left. Wrist cc, Sergeant?"

Kartr did not start at the abrupt change in the other's speach. He knew that Rolth was at the door behind him.

"Medico Tre, Ranger Rolth." He was careful to glance around before making the introduction. No need to tip off Tre that he was a sensitive.

The medico acknowledged the Faltharian's salute. "Pleased to see you, ranger. Any aches or pains to report? Goggles holding up? Need any skin burn cream? You *are* a Faltharian?"

The lips below Rolth's goggle mask curved into a smile which expanded under the medico's friendliness. "You know all about my problems then, Medico?"

"Had a Faltharian patient once—bad skin burn. That's what started me messing around with creams. Found one which did help a lot. Wait a minute—"

He hurried to a medicine case in the corner and began checking over the assortment of plaso-tubes it held. "Try this." He brought out one. "Spread it on before you go into direct daylight. I think you will find it will stop irritation."

"Thanks, Medico." Rolth put the tube into his belt pouch. "So far I've been cc. Only the sergeant here had work for you."

Kartr flipped his left hand up and down from the restored wrist. "And this is as good as new. What's your fee?"

Tre laughed. "Credit slips wouldn't have much value

here, would they? If you come across anything interesting in my line when you go exploring, just let me know. That will be good enough for me. Glad to be of service to the Patrol at any time, anyway. You boys deserve the best we civilians can give you. I hear that you may be hunting— any chance of going along some time on one of your trips?"

Kartr was surprised. There was an urgency in that question and the medico's eyes locked with his as if Tre were trying desperately to tell him something—a message vitally important to both of them.

"I don't see why not," the sergeant returned. "If we do go. I've had no orders as yet. Thanks again, Medico—"

"Not at all. Only too glad to be able to help. See you around—"

But still underneath that urgent appeal. Then Kartr's eyes widened. The fingers of the medico's right hand— they had moved—were moving again—to shape a figure he knew well. But how—how and when had Tre learned that? Automatically he made the prescribed answer with his forefinger, even as he said loudly:

"If and when we go out, we'll let you know. Clear skies—"

"Clear skies." The other returned the spaceman's good-bye.

Outside the door Kartr's hand closed for a moment only on Rolth's. The Faltharian at once began talking about hunting.

"Those horned beasts we saw in the clearing," he said as they mounted the stairs again, "they should make excellent eating. There may be some way of salting down the flesh—if we could locate salt deposits. And the same for those river creatures Zinga is always talking about. We needn't send him to bring in those." The Faltharian laughed as light-heartedly as if he had not caught the

110

message and was speaking now for other ears. "He'd eat more than he'd bring back."

"We'd better not use the blasters," Kartr cut in as if he were giving some serious thought to the question. "Spoils too much of the meat. Force blades—"

"Have to get in close to use them, wouldn't you?" asked Rolth dubiously.

Both of them were climbing faster. There was someone behind them now. Kartr's mind touched and then recoiled, sickened. The Can-hound was trailing them. But they did not run, though they were breathing hard when they reached the top of the last flight and saw the door to the tower open just far enough for them to squeeze through. Zinga slammed it shut on their heels with an open-jawed snarl of rage.

"So that's after you!"

"As a trailer only, I think. Let him stew around outside. Now, Rolth, what about that woman. What did she want?"

"She thought we were brave heroes come to the rescue. Cummi's kept it dark—our arrival—but word got around—our uniforms are too well known. She came to ask for help. The situation here is just about what you thought it was. Cummi's set himself up as a pocket-sized Central Control. You do just as he says or you don't eat. And if you protest too loudly you disappear—"

"How many have disappeared?" Fylh wanted to know.

"The Captain of the *X451* and three or four others. Then there were four Bemmy passengers—they disappeared too. But not in the same way. I gather that they saw which way the stars were showing right after the landing and went off into the blue by themselves—"

"Bemmys! What species?" Zinga's frill made a fan behind his head. He still stood by the door as if listening to something on the other side of the portal.

"I couldn't get that out of her. She didn't see them until after the ship came down—it was a two-class liner. Anyway there is now a Cummi party, small but armed and dangerous, and an anti-Cummi party badly organized and just milling around—taking it out in talk where they can't be overheard by the lord and master. Cummi himself keeps holed up here and has his men patrolling. Those who know anything—the techneers, the medico— he keeps right under his eyes. That Can-hound is one of his big threats."

"Are we invited to join the anti-Cummi party?" Fylh asked.

"I don't think it has gone that far yet. They had an idea that the Patrol had moved in to take over. And do you know—I think that that is just what we might have done if we had handled this the way you wanted to, Kartr—allowed them to think we had an undamaged ship and were on duty. I had to tell the woman that we were not in charge. But I also informed her that the rangers were sticking together."

"They may plan a palace revolution," Kartr mused. "Very well. I say we stick tight here until we know more."

"Where did that medico learn ranger hand talk?" Rolth wondered.

"A question I'll ask him if I ever get the chance. He's another who suggested the waiting game and to keep our eyes open and our mouths shut."

"Our eyes and other things open—" Zinga's head was pressed against the surface of the door. "The Can-hound is about to do a little prying. Think sweet thoughts for him—quick!"

# 9

## SHOWDOWN

"Then you press this little knob and— Neat, isn't it?"

Kartr had to agree with the Zacathan that the results of pressing the little knob were neat. Water, clear, honest, fresh water splashed out of a spout disguised as a monster's head and fell into a basin set in the floor, a basin large enough to accommodate with ease even Kartr's inches.

"Go on—try it!" urged Zinga. "I did—twice! And you don't see me any the worse for it, do you?" He turned slowly around flexing his muscles and grinning toothily.

Rolth leaned back against the edge of the doorway and watched the flood suspiciously.

"What about the water supply? Could our friends down below shut it off if they wanted to?"

Kartr had unbuckled and thrown aside belt and tunic. Now he paused uncertainly. It might be wiser to conserve water instead of wasting it on baths. But the Zacathan shook his head.

"The pipes carrying this run up through the walls. If they shut us off they will probably have to shut off their own supply also. Anyway—if a siege is included in their future plans we'd be fools to allow ourselves to get bottled up here any longer than it would take us to climb down

113

that outer wall. Don't be a spoilsport," he ended. "Or do you *like* to go dirty?"

Kartr peeled off the rest of his clothing and kicked it across the floor. He had one clean outfit in his bag and he reveled in the thought of using it.

"I wonder what they looked like—" He tried the temperature of the pool with his toes and found it to be pleasantly warm—much more comfortable than the mountain stream.

"Who—? Oh, you mean the builders of this delightful spot? Well"—Zinga indicated the mirrored walls—"they were not ashamed to look themselves in the face. Wonder if those ever before reflected any bathers as ugly as you two—"

Kartr laughed and splashed water at the Zacathan "Speak for yourself, Zinga. I'll have you know that my face is not considered suitable for frightening children—"

Or did that still hold true, he wondered suddenly, and for the first time surveyed his reflection critically as it appeared in the mirror which ran the full length of the wall behind the basin.

The deep brown skin which proclaimed his space-borne occupation had only a few lines as yet. Of course, above that dark expanse the color of his hair did look rather odd. But its soft cream and red brown in waving strips was perfectly natural for a son of Ylene. He had two eyes, green, set slightly aslant—a straight nose—a mouth centrally placed—all proper for a human.

"Teeth too small—"

Kartr flushed and watched the dark crimson creep up along his sharply defined cheek bones.

"Freeze and blast you, Zinga! Can't you leave a man's thoughts alone?"

"Admiring himself, was he? But I don't agree about the teeth—large ones aren't marks of beauty among our kind, you know—"

114

Zinga was standing open-jawed just before his own section of mirror. "And why not? Useful and beautiful both. I'd like to see either of you two puny humans take part in one of our warrior duels—no talons—no proper teeth— you wouldn't last a minute!"

"Beauty is in the eye of the beholder and conditioned by upbringing," announced the Faltharian. "Now Kartr's people have two-shaded hair—so does their ideal of beauty. My race"—he had been shedding helmet and tunic as he talked—"have white hair, white skin—pale eyes. So—for us those attributes are necessary to be considered handsome."

"Oh, you are all answers to the sighs of maidens." Fylh's voice deflated from the doorway. "Why not finish up that absurd splashing about in liquid and come and eat. Such a stupid waste of time—"

But Kartr refused to be hurried and Rolth was as leisurely in enjoying Zinga's discovery. When they were again clad and followed Fylh into the outer room they found the Trystian curled up on the ledge of an open window exchanging trills with several large birds.

"Gossiping again," commented Zinga. "And where is this food that it was so important that we eat? I'll wager two credits that he's passed it out to those feathered friends of his!"

"Serve you right if I had. But you'll find it just beyond your noses."

The concentrated rations were twice as tasteless to anyone who had recently dined on roasted meat and the fresh fruits of the wilderness. Kartr chewed and swallowed conscientiously and longed to return to the past.

"I'll take it back." Zinga gagged realistically after he downed the last cube. "Fylh wouldn't pass this offal on— it would kill the birds and he likes birds—"

"What are we doing here anyway?" There was the whir of wings as the birds went and Fylh dropped to the floor, closing the window. "We should have stayed out there. This is a dead place and there is no sense in trying to bring it to life!"

"Don't worry. We'll probably be outside again sooner than we bargain for. Let's go down and agree to go hunting like good little rangers and then go—and never come back!"

Kartr looked up. He could understand that plea of Zinga's, and part of him wanted to do just what the Zacathan suggested. And he could participate in Fylh's feeling that this was a dead place returned to an unnatural life. But—there were women and children below in the city and there was a cold season approaching—unless Cummi had lied about that also. Maybe the intal planters, and some of the other passengers had hunted, but could their efforts supply all the needs of the community? And that woman today, she had appealed to Rolth, believed in their help just because they wore the Comets.

"It is like this," the sergeant began slowly, trying to put all these tangled feelings into the right words, to spread out before the others both sides of the question. "Do we have any right to walk out when we may be needed? On the other hand, if Cummi's anti-Bemmy talk puts you two in danger, you must go—"

"Why—?"

Zinga interrupted Fylh. "We don't go yet. But I see your point. Only, let me warn you, Kartr, there are times when a man—or a Bemmy—has to harden his heart. We needn't make any decisions tonight. A good rest—"

"Locked door or not, I'm suggesting a watch," Fylh stated.

"They won't try to reach us—that way." Kartr shook his head.

"You mean—mind touch!" Rolth whistled. "Then Fylh and I won't be much help."

"True. So Zinga and I will divide the night."

There followed uneasy hours. Three rolled in bedrolls, one on guard, slipping on unbooted feet from room to room, up and down, listening with both ears and mind. They did it in two-hour watches and Kartr had taken to his bed for the second time when Zinga hailed him with a low hiss. The sergeant pulled out with a sigh to join the Zacathan at an open window.

"Smitt is coming—across that other roof—"

The Zacathan was right; the mind pattern of the com-techneer identified him. And only a trained ranger could have sighted him. His dodging from shadow to shadow, his use of every bit of cover was Patrol work at its best.

"I'll go down to meet him." Before Zinga could protest Kartr was through the window and on that ladder of block design. Fortunately it was a cloudy night and he thought that unless someone were watching him through vision lenses he could not be seen, his uniform being almost the same shade as the stone.

As the sergeant came within a foot or two of the roof over which Smitt was advancing he gave a soft whistle of Patrol recognition. There was a moment of silence and then he was answered and the com-techneer came running to join him.

"Kartr here—"

"Thank the Spirit of Space! I've been trying to reach you for hours!"

"What's up?"

"The men—those against Cummi. They've taken our appearance here as a signal to fight him. The idiotic fools! He has a disruptor mounted in every main corridor, they can't get anywhere near him. And that Can-hound has knocked out two of the leaders—put them to sleep the same way you did Snyn back in the ship. It'll be nothing but raw murder if they try to storm Cummi's quarters! He had Jaksan locked up with the medico—and the techneers are under guard. He'll wipe out all opposition—"

"What plans does he have for us?"

"He's planted a force bomb at the foot of your tower stairs. If you try to come down—finish! And he and the Can-hound are cooking up something special to smoke you out—"

Something special! If the Arcturian believed that he was only dealing with a sensitive of equal powers there were many things he could try. But against a six point six AND Zinga such attacks might backfire.

"I've got to get back." Smitt nursed his blaster in one hand. "I've got to keep those fools from attacking head on. Is there anything you can do?"

"I don't know. But we'll try. Hold off your men as long as you can. Maybe we can turn tables—"

Smitt melted away into the night. If he kept his mental guard he was going to be a formidable addition to the rebel forces. Neither the Arcturian nor the Can-hound could get to him that way. Kartr climbed back up to the tower window to discover all the rangers waiting for him.

"That was Smitt." As usual darkness had not confused Rolth. "What did he want?"

"There's a rebellion against Cummi. The other side took our arrival for the signal to break loose."

"And Cummi, of course, has not been slumbering peacefully meanwhile. What have his merry men prepared for us?"

"Yes"—Rolth added his question to Fylh's—"what is ready and waiting for us?"

"Smitt said a force bomb at the foot of the stairs, ready to go off as we go down—"

"Play rough, don't they? Do you know, I think that

118

somebody should put the old healthy fear of the Patrol into these gentlemen—"

"Where's Zinga?" Kartr interrupted the Faltharian.

"Gone below to do what he calls 'listening.' " Fylh laid a torch on the floor, pulled the edge of his bedroll partially over it and by the shielded light began to count out the extra clips for their blasters. It did not, unfortunately, take him very long to finish the task.

"That all we have?" Kartr asked grimly.

"You have the charges now in your weapons and the extras in your belt loops—if you've followed regulations. These are the rest."

"All right. It comes to three apiece and the one over for Rolth. If this is to be a night fight we might as well give the advantage to the one who can make the best use of it."

The Faltharian was busy at a task of his own, securing their packs. If they did not have to make a run for it, they might be able to bring off their equipment too.

"They've moved our sled into the hallway down there and it is probably under guard now. If we win though—"

"If we win," Fylh broke in, "we can march right in and take it. We might just do that anyway. What's keeping the old lizard?"

Kartr had wondered about that, too, enough to send a questing thought which was answered instantly with a strong impression of danger. The sergeant scooped up his share of the blaster clips and tucked them into his belt before he crossed the room and went down to the green fish chamber. Zinga stood pressed against the door as if he wished to melt into its surface. Kartr joined him to "listen."

There were movements—not too far away—maybe just beyond the foot of the staircase. Two living things withdrew, a third remained—that was the Can-hound. But why did they leave that one on guard unless—

Unless, Zinga's thought answered him in a second's flash, they suspect that you—or I—are not what we seem. But they cannot know the full truth or they would not leave the Can-hound. Not after the way you handled him before. They must never have discovered that—

Or is he—bait? Kartr thought back to Zinga, reveling in the freedom of this exchange which he had always longed to experience but had never found before.

That we shall see. This time the task is mine—brother!

Kartr withdrew mind touch and concentrated only on trying to sense the approach of any other who might break Zinga's control. He felt the Zacathan's body grow tense and guessed the agony Zinga was feeling.

It was as if they had stepped out of time—planet time. Kartr never knew how long they fought their soundless battle before he had to give a warning.

"One comes." He said that aloud, not daring to break in by thought.

Zinga hissed a long sigh. "He *was* bait of a sort," he answered in words, as if his thought power was almost exhausted. "But not as we had feared. He has been under observation all the time—if he withdrew against orders then they could assume that we were powerful enough to control him. So they suspect—but they do not know."

"You say—they—we face more than Cummi and the Can-hound?"

"Cummi has learned to tap the mind energy of some others—how many I do not know. If a five point nine can do that—"

"What will he be able to raise himself to?" A great deal of Kartr's confidence was wiped out by the thought of that. Even with Zinga could he face down a Cummi so reinforced?

"I suggest," Zinga said a little dryly as if he were shaken also, "that we continue to stick to blasters as of-
120

fensive weapons for a while. That way the odds are easier to assess."

"And we'll have to get out of here to be able to use those. If we leave, that thing below will know it at once."

"Which leaves us only one answer—we'll have to split up for now. You and Rolth take the outside route down and see what you can do in the general melee. Fylh and I shall hold the fort and try to make two think as four."

Kartr could see the wisdom in that. As humans Rolth and he would have a better chance of getting co-operation from the rebels. At the same time the Bemmy scouts would be safe from ruthless shooting.

The climb down to the roof top across which Smitt had come was ridiculously easy. They paused there long enough to pull on their boots, and then snaked over it from shadow to shadow. When they reached the parapet Rolth looked over. Then he dropped back and put his lips close to Kartr's ear.

"One floor below there is a ledge. It leads to a lighted window. The drop is sheer, I do not think that anyone who may be in that room would expect company to arrive through the window—"

"And how do you reach the ledge?"

"Our belts hooked together and passed around this— here—" The Faltharian put his hand on a tooth-shaped projection ornamenting the parapet.

If Kartr had an instant picture of what it meant to dangle so precariously over the edge of a sheer drop he did not betray himself.

"It is good that we are both tall." Rolth buckled his belt to the one the sergeant reluctantly passed over. "A short man could not make it."

The Faltharian slipped the loop in one end of his improvised rope over the projection and climbed over the parapet. Holding his body at an angle he half slid, half walked down the stone. Kartr huddled against the edge and forced himself to watch. Then Rolth stopped and the belt swung loosely in the sergeant's fingers.

Not so skillfully as Rolth, Kartr made the same trip, keeping his eyes fast on the stone before him, trying not to think of the darkness below. He inched downward for an eternity and then Rolth's hand pulled him straight and his boots touched the path of the ledge. He found that it was wider than it appeared from above, he could get all but a small scrap of heel onto it.

"Anyone in the room?" Rolth demanded as they crept toward the window.

Kartr sent out the probe. "Not in the room—near though—"

The Faltharian answered that with a ghost of laughter. "We're almost as good as some of Fylh's feathered friends. Here goes!" He caught at the window frame and pulled himself against it, jamming open the casement with his knee. It gave with a faint squeak of protest and Rolth landed lightly on his feet within where Kartr joined him a second later.

They were in a chamber where someone was at home. A pile of bedding lay on a bunk bed which had been obviously torn out of ship's fittings. Two expensive Valcunite luggage bags stood against the wall and a table, also ship use, was piled almost to the sagging point with personal belongings.

Rolth's nostrils wrinkled. "What a stink!" he commented under his breath.

Kartr tried to remember where he had smelled that too sweet cura blossom fragrance before.

"Fortus Kan!" When they had run against the secretary in the corridor that morning he had certainly carried cura lily with him.

And as if that identification had been either a summons or an entrance cue, the Vice-Sector Lord's man was coming toward them now. Kartr had warning enough to plaster himself back against the wall by the door, and Rolth, seeing his move, did the same on the other side of the portal.

There was apprehension to be read in the mind of the man who was fumbling with the intricate ancient fastening. Fortus Kan was afraid. The fastening was defying him, too, so that exasperation began to drown out the fear. He lost command enough to kick the panel as it gave. With such a medley of emotions uncovered it would be easy for Kartr to—

The sergeant allowed him four steps into the room before he put the flat of his hand against the door and sent it shut again. Fortus Kan spun around—to face the small and deadly mouths of two Patrol blasters. And at the sight all his resistance crumbled at once.

"Please!" His hands went up to his working mouth. He retreated backward, without looking where he going, until the cot caught him behind the knees and he plumped down upon it as if he were as boneless as a Lydia V creature.

As Kartr walked toward him the little man cringed as if he wanted to burrow into the tangle of bedding.

"One would begin to think, Kartr, that this gentleman has a guilty conscience—"

Rolth's words might have been the lash of a Centurian slaver's whip the way Fortus Kan reacted. He stopped trying to pull himself under the covers and sat stone still, his mouth trembling, his eyes glassy with—Kartr recognized—pure fear.

"Please—" The secretary had to work to get that one word out, but it was a stopper which had held up the flood. "Please—I had nothing to do with it—nothing! I advised him not to antagonize the Patrol. I know the law— Why, I have a second cousin who is the clerk in your administration office on Sexti. I wouldn't go against

123

the Patrol—never. I had nothing, absolutely nothing to do with it!"

His fear was so rank that it was almost an odor in the room. But what was he afraid of—the planting of the force bomb, that trick with the Can-hound? There was only one way to get at the full truth. And for the second time in his life Kartr ruthlessly invaded a fellow human's mind, breaking down the feeble block, exploring, learning what he wanted—in part. Fortus Kan whimpered, was quiet. He would be quiet for a while now. Kartr turned away. There was a lot to do. A pity that Cummi had not trusted the little man more, there were such big gaps in his information—gaps which might be fatal if the rangers were not careful.

The sergeant came back to Rolth. "There's a force bomb under the tower stairs, all right. And the Can-hound is set to trick us out and blow it up. Everyone is being moved out of the top floors here before it goes off. Kan came back for some precious personal possessions. The stairs is under guard—"

"We could blast through—rather noisy though."

"Yes. One thing I'm wondering about—why all these staircases when they had gravity wells, too. Odd—maybe important."

"This was a state building," Rolth reminded him. "Might use stairs for reasons of ceremony. Like those Opolti who fly everywhere except in the Affid's quarter. No evidence of any other way down from here. What about the boys? If that Can-hound gets tired of waiting for them to come out he may just set the bomb off anyway and trust to luck to bag the game."

"Yes—"

Kartr stood stiffly. He was blacking out, first the corridors, then this room, his awareness of Rolth, of Fortus Kan, of his own person. He did it! His mind touched Zinga's! He gave the warning. Then he was back in the

124

frowzy room, shaking his head dazedly, to see Rolth crouched by the door listening. Men—two—three of them were coming along the hall outside—straight for this room!

# 10

## *BATTLE*

**A sharp rap on the door froze both rangers.**

"Kan! We're moving out now. Come along!"

But Fortus Kan was deep in a world of his own.

"Kan! You fool, come on!"

Kartr made mind contact. Out there was the young ship's officer he had met early in the day, two others—human, non-sensitive. They were impatient, impatient because of fear. And the fear won out. After some garbled conversation, which came through the door only as a murmur, they went on. Rolth glided to the window and studied what lay below.

"I take it that we have to move fast?" he asked without turning around.

"They were afraid—too afraid to linger very long. What's below?"

"Another roof outcrop, but so far down we couldn't hope to make it without a climber's sucker pads."

"We have a substitute for sucker pads." Kartr rolled Fortus Kan off the bed and set to work tearing its coverings into strips which Rolth caught up and knotted together. Working against time, but testing each knot, they produced a rough rope.

"You first," ordered the sergeant. "Then this." He touched Kan with the toe of his boot. "I'll come last.

Over now—time must be running out fast or they wouldn't have been in such a hurry to clear out."

Rolth was gone almost before he finished speaking. Kartr hung over the window sill to watch but the Faltharian was so quickly hidden in the dark that only the movements of the rope told when he stopped climbing down and signaled a safe landing. Kartr pulled the clumsy line back into the room, his palms wet against the torn cloth. There was a terrible urgency goading him. He tied the cloth loop under Kan's arms and manhandled the secretary's limp body over the sill, lowering it as slowly as he could until a sharp jerk told him Rolth was in charge. Kartr did not even wait until Kan was untied before he was descending hand over hand.

And as his feet hit the surface of the roof below it happened. There was no sound at first. But the support under him danced. He fell flat and buried his head in his arms, not daring to watch what was happening above. Force bomb all right. He had once before been caught in the backwash of one. Had Zinga and Fylh escaped in time? Resolutely he shut that fear out of his mind. There was a faint moan from Kan. Rolth—?

But on the edge of that thought came the Faltharian's voice.

"Quite a display! Cummi likes to play rough, doesn't he?"

The sergeant sat up. He was trembling—perhaps with reaction from that frenzied descent—but, he decided, mostly from the black rage which possessed him now whenever he thought of the Arcturian. A rage he must best or that other sensitive could turn it into a weapon against him.

"How do we get away from here?" He must depend on Rolth's ability to pierce the gloom. For it was real gloom which walled them in now. The dancing lights of the city

127

were gone—they were crouched in the middle of a black blot.

"Window over there—not too high to reach. What about this prize package? Do we have to lug him along?"

"He'll wake by morning. Get him inside a room and leave him. I don't think they'll try another bomb."

"Not unless they want to bring the whole place down around their heads. Let's go. If you'll take Kan's legs, I'll heave his head."

Kartr stumbled along, trusting to Rolth to guide them. They reached a window, beat open the casement and crawled through with their unconscious burden.

"Aren't we in the wrong building now?" the sergeant wanted to know. "I thought we climbed down over there—"

"You're right. We're in a different one. But this was the easiest and quickest route out. Did the boys get away?"

For the second time Kartr tried to reach Zinga—sent out those shafts of thought. Once—for a single joyful second he thought he had made contact—then it was gone. He dared not try too long, the Can-hound—if that creature still lived—or even Cummi might be able to pick up his signal.

"No use," he told Rolth. "I can't make contact. But that doesn't mean we have to worry. They may be too far away—we've never been able to discover what governs mental reception or how far we can beam a call. And they may be lying low because the Arcturian is too near. But I did reach Zinga before the blast and they had several minutes more than we did to escape."

That was not much to pin any hope to, Kartr knew that. But with such veterans as Fylh and Zinga it was almost enough.

"Do we try to locate Smitt?"

"I think so. Or at least we can make contact with his rebels."

Kartr hooked his fingers in Rolth's belt and allowed the Faltharian to tow him through dark rooms and darker hallways, while he tried to keep some sense of direction.

"Street level," came the welcome whisper at last.

"I believe that we are facing the street which runs along the front of Cummi's headquarters—"

But, before Rolth could affirm or deny that, a brilliant bolt of fire snapped across the dark and both of them involuntarily ducked.

A blaster shot! And that was another from down the street. A third beam brought a choked, horrible scream in answer.

"The war's on!" Rolth pointed out unnecessarily. "And which is our side?"

"Neither, just yet. I don't want to guess wrong and be fried," returned Kartr grimly. "There's one to our left— about five feet away— He's crawling past us at an angle. I'll try contact as he goes by and see who he is—"

The lashes of fire continued to light up the sod-grown street at intervals. There were no more cries so either the aim continued to be poor, or very, very good.

The sniper crawled across their vantage point.

"No uniform," Rolth reported. "Looks like a civilian to me. But he knows blasters. Maybe the veteran of a sector war—"

"He's not a Cummi man but—" Kartr had no time for a warning.

No, the man out there was not one of Cummi's followers, but he had caught that tentative mind touch in an instant—something which had never happened to Kartr before. And his blaster swung around at the rangers.

"Patrol!" Rolth yelled.

The blaster aim wavered, and then held steady at them.

"Come out—with your hands up!" ordered a harsh

voice. "I've set this on 'spray' and I'll use it that way, too!"

Kartr and Rolth obeyed, hunking forward at a half stoop for there were other blasters busy farther down.

"Who in Space are you?" demanded their captor.

"Patrol rangers. We're trying to contact Smitt, our com-techneer—"

"Yeah?" There was deep suspicion in that voice. "Well, you're going to contact him now. Get going down in that direction and I'm right behind you if you try to run—"

They followed orders which brought them to a dark doorway some distance away.

"Stairs here," Rolth informed his companion.

"Sure," agreed the man behind them. "Go down them, and shut up!"

But five steps down brought them to a barrier.

"Knock on that four times quick, wait a second and knock again!" came the order of their guard.

Rolth obeyed and the portal moved aside. They blundered through a thick curtain and found themselves in a dimly lighted hall where two men eyed them with no pretense of friendship and a blaster was pointed at their middles. But when the light touched their comets there came recognition and relaxation. One of the guardians stepped closer.

"Take off your helmets," he commanded.

The rangers obeyed and then blinked as a torch beam centered on them.

"It's cc. They're not Cummi's—they must be Patrol. Take them in to Krowli. How is it going topside?"

"We lie on our bellies and shoot—they do the same. At least we knocked out the robots' signal cables so they can't turn those against us again. Far as I can see it's stalemate," their late captor replied. "Cc. Let the old man out, boys—back to the firing line!"

"Get one of the igits for me, Pol!"

"I'll do that little thing. Fry him on a platter. Good landing!"

"And clear skies!" One of the guards closed the door and rearranged the folds of the improvised blackout curtain. The other jerked a thumb at the rangers.

"Down this way."

They went down the length of the hallway into a large room which was the scene of some activity. Several men squatted around some boxes digging machinery parts out of packing. Two others sat at a box table and three more were making a scratch meal at the far end of the room. The newcomers were waved toward the two at the table. One of them raised his head and then jumped to his feet. It was Smitt.

"It is stalemate all right." The com-techneer ran his fingers through his hair.

Kartr and Rolth studied the crude map which lay on the table top.

"We have them bottled up in the headquarters building. By the way, did they blow the tower? We felt some sort of a shock—"

The sergeant nodded without replying aloud. "If Cummi has disruptors," he said, "I don't see why he lets a handful of snipers pen him in. He could blow himself a path out any time he wants to."

"Well." The slim, middle-aged man who shared Smitt's table when the rangers had been brought in, stretched and grinned. "Cummi doesn't want to blow big holes in his nice city, not if he can help it. And snipers are hard to locate."

"Not for a sensitive," Kartr pointed out. "Give me five minutes out there and I can tag every one of your men. Cummi need only send out the Can-hound and—"

Krowli's grin vanished as if wiped off by a brutal hand. "You have a point there, Sergeant," he admitted in a voice of mild tone, but the emotions seething below it were anything but mild.

"Could it be," Rolth struck in, "that disruptor shells are not too many in Lord Cummi's armory?"

"That thought has also occurred to us," Krowli answered. "Only it is a little difficult to prove. Cummi has had all the arms under his control since the second day we landed. We have only personal side arms which he could not logically take from us. This whole rotten mess came about just because he was able to think faster than the rest of us. And be sure that he didn't overlook the point of holding all the guns he could! We might storm Cummi's headquarters, sure, but if the disruptors do work—that would be the end of the stormers. And he has two sensitives—we have—"

"Two also, if I can contact Zinga. Any more among your people?"

Krowli shook his head. "We are—were—about as ordinary a crowd of average citizens as you could find anywhere in Control territory. Cummi grabbed all those of use to him, along with the arms."

Rolth had been studying the map and now he dug a fingernail into the center of the square representing Cummi's hold.

"I notice you don't have the tube-tunnel marked—"

"What tube-tunnel?" Krowli wanted to know.

Smitt smashed his fist down on the box and swore at the pain. "I'm three kinds of a Domanti idiot," he shouted. And then Kartr's explanation interrupted him.

"It depends now upon whether Cummi has discovered those underground routes," the sergeant concluded.

"He doesn't know of them—I'm almost certain of that! None of us heard of them before—unless the techneers have discovered them and kept the secret."

Rolth looked up. "If they did just that we may be leading a forlorn hope right into a stinger's nest."

"And if they don't know"—Smitt was almost exultant—"we'll be in their midst before they are aware of it!"

"You've got to pick the right men for this," Kartr warned without any of Smitt's enthusiasm. "You're the right type, Smitt. They can't crack your mind shield. But the rest—we'll have to have men with whom the Canhound and Cummi can't tamper. Now take that fellow who brought us in—he isn't a sensitive, at least he doesn't seem to be, yet he caught my thought beam and jumped us at once."

"That must have been Norgot. He has had good reason to learn how to protect himself against mind invasion. He was one of the Satsati hostages—"

"So!" Rolth paid tribute. "No wonder he was edgy when you tried to probe him, Kartr. He ought to be a perfect choice for the boarding party."

"Boarding party!" thought Kartr fleetingly. Odd how the space terms stuck in their speech even now when they were permanently earthed.

"Yes," he said aloud. "Any more of his caliber around?"

Krowli beckoned to one of the men who had just finished eating. "You're a sensitive, Sergeant. We'll leave the selection up to you."

In the end they assembled eight men with mind shields tight enough to make them possibilities. Kartr longed for Zinga and Fylh, but so far nothing had been heard from the Bemmy rangers, although the rebel patrols had been alerted to keep watch for them.

Together the party of ten descended one by one in the gravity well the rangers had first discovered. There was a single car at the platform and three were a very tight fit for the voyage. But they made it that way, with Rolth at the controls each trip forward and back. And at last they stood near the plate elevator under Cummi's headquarters. Kartr could see no indication that there had been any visitors there since the time he and the Faltharian had passed that way before.

It was those two other stops along the way, the ones they had sped by then, which interested him now. If there was any welcoming party waiting for them at the top of the shaft it might be well to make an earlier stop. So he pushed the lowest button on the wall. The five of them who had managed to crowd on the plate clung together as they were whisked up.

Their support came to a stop in darkness and Kartr marshaled his four companions off to let the elevator sink back. Then he dared to flash his beam about.

They were on a ledge from which a ramp ran up into the darkness. Underfoot was a coating of fine, gritty dust which Kartr believed had not been disturbed for centuries. And there was no indication of life other than their own, his perception assured him of that. Cummi must be ignorant of this breach in his defenses.

The swish of displaced air heralded the arrival of the plate again and then Smitt, Rolth and the other three rebels joined them. Rolth hung out over the well and surveyed the space overhead.

"Cc. It closed up when the plate hit bottom. Unless someone was up there watching at just this moment they'll never know."

Kartr switched off his torch and Rolth took the lead, each man grasping hold of the belt of the one before him, forming a chain to negotiate the dark through which only Rolth could pass freely. At first the angle of the ramp was a steep one, but it began to level off until they found themselves in a large room, coming around the base of a partition into a lighted space filled with the buzz of running machinery. The partition from this side seemed solid wall and Kartr did not wonder that the ramp and the shaft it led to had not been discovered. At the same instant he not only became aware of a man ahead but was able to identify him.

"Dalgre!"

The sergeant beckoned to Smitt. "Dalgre's ahead—with another—maybe a guard, unless he has joined Cummi. You might have better luck contacting him than I would. And I can cover you—"

The com-techneer replied with a short nod and signaled to his rebel followers to stay where they were. Then, together with Kartr, he ran from the shadow of one giant machine to another, until they were able to see into a pool of brighter light where Dalgre sat before the board of controls and a man in the rumpled uniform of a jetman lounged several feet away, a force beam projector cradled in his arm.

Kartr touched Smitt's shoulder and pointed to himself and then to the left, a path which would, with continued luck, bring him near the guard. He took it, moving like a gray wisp of fog around machines whose purpose he could not guess, until he came up behind the jetman. From where he crouched he could see the tip of Smitt's helmet ridge crest.

Then the com-techneer stepped boldly out and in that same instant Kartr sprang, bringing the butt of his blaster down on the guard's right arm. The man screamed and doubled up against the side of the control board, dropping the projector which flew across the floor. In a second Dalgre had scooped it up and was in a half crouch ready to fire. But Smitt's familiar grays were in his sights and he did not squeeze the trigger.

"Very neat," commented the com-techneer. "One would think you had practiced it. I take it that you are *not* a convert to Cummi, Dalgre?"

The Patrolman showed his teeth. "Is that likely? They needed me—so I'm still alive. But they blasted Snyn and the Commander—maybe Jaksan also for all I know—"

"What?" all three of the Patrol demanded almost with a single voice.

"Did it an hour ago. Last I heard Jaksan and the medico were barricaded in the west wing. This is a madhouse. About time we put some fear for the comet back into these space-blasted igits! If it weren't for the Can-hound being able to find out where everyone is and what he's doing, I'd have tried to make a break before this—"

The jetman guard was tied with his own belt to the legs of the bench before the control board. Kartr looked over the array of dials there.

"Anything you can do to this that might put the odds in our favor?"

Dalgre grinned ruefully. "I'm afraid to chance it. I'm no real mech-techneer. And they gave me only a half hour's briefing before they put me here. If I pull the wrong lever I might blow us up. Too bad—because we might be able to shake them right out of the building if we only knew what all those gadgets mean."

"How do you get out of here?" one of the rebels wanted to know.

"Anti-gravity lift." Dalgre guided them to an alcove beyond the control board. "Only trouble is that they may have a guard on the upper level who will become suspicious if we rise before my shift is up."

"And how long will that be?"

Dalgre consulted his wrist dial. "A full half hour, planet time."

"Can't wait that long," Kartr decided. "Any other stops on this rise beside the one you are supposed to use?"

"No."

"But there is something else—" Rolth had been examining the walls of the shaft. "Here are holds for hands and feet—perhaps to be used in times of emergency. We can climb out—"

And climb they did. Kartr caught the message of a

stranger ahead—the guard Dalgre had predicted. It was also Dalgre who had the answer.

"Let me hail him—"

The sergeant pulled back against the side of the well and kept only a single handhold on the climbing bars as the other Patrolman squeezed by him. A moment later they heard Dalgre hail whoever was at the top.

"Give us a hand—"

"What's the matter?"

"I'm no mech-techneer—send for one of your fellows—one of these blasted machines down here is running wild. It may blow us up or something!"

Dalgre climbed the last few feet out of the shaft and moved away from its mouth.

"Where's Taleng? Why didn't he come up with the message?" The guard was openly suspicious.

"Because—" Kartr heard Dalgre start to answer and then came sounds of a struggle.

The sergeant swarmed up the last rungs and out of the hole. Dalgre was fighting with the guard for the possession of a hand force beam. Kartr did not try to reach his feet but sent his body plunging forward to bring down both men. They fell on him with force enough to drive the air out of his lungs in an agonized grunt.

Minutes later the foggy scene began to clear again. The guard lay bound and gagged close to the wall and Rolth kneeled beside the sergeant kneading Kartr's ribs to force the air back into him again. Smitt, Dalgre and the rebels had vanished. Rolth replied to the question the sergeant did not yet have breath enough to ask.

"I couldn't hold them back."

"But—" Kartr's words came between painful gasps, "Cummi—the Can-hound—"

"They don't honestly believe very much in danger from a sensitive's power," Rolth reminded him. "Even if they have seen a demonstration—they simply refuse to believe the evidence presented by their eyes. It's the way most humans are made—"

"How very true. Luckily for us—"

Kartr froze and did not finish his sentence. Instead he turned on Rolth and sent the Faltharian sprawling forward into a doorway beyond. "Get out there quick and see if you can stop those fools making targets of themselves. I know that there's trouble waiting for them ahead—"

He watched Rolth pick himself up and go. Because the trouble wasn't ahead he hoped that the Faltharian would not stop to ask questions. There was trouble, right enough, but it lay behind, coming closer every second.

Cummi was coming—and this time Kartr knew that it was to be battle between them, an all-out battle without quarter on either side—a battle fought on no visible field and for an untellable victory.

# 11
## OUTCAST

Kartr was lying on his back, staring up into a leaden sky, and fine needles of rain stung eyes and skin. The cold was numbing and from somewhere nearby came a whimpering. After long minutes he knew that he was the whimperer. But he could not stop the sound, any more than he could control the shudders which shook his whole aching body. He willed his hands to move and they dragged heavily aross torn clothing and patches of raw flesh.

Then he tried to sit up. His head swam sickeningly and the gray world whirled around. But he could see rocks, scrubby bushes ringing him in. His mind sorted the evidence of his eyes, as he watched blood ooze sluggishly from a cut along his ribs. He accepted the reality of the pain in his body, the stone ledge on which he lay, and the bushes— All were a part of this world—

This world? What world?

That question brought to life a white-hot fire in his mind. He cringed and tried not to think as the rain washed the blood away from his chest. He was almost content as long as he did not think. There was a second thrust of agony through his head as he became aware of other life near. A tawny muzzle broke through the bushes, round yellow animal eyes regarded him unwaveringly, a cold curiosity touched his mind. He sent a silent appeal to it for aid—and the head vanished.

Then he moaned and his clumsy hands caught his spinning head. For he knew now that for him there was no help. Behind him lay a barrier which cut him off from the past. He shrank from the torture that edge of memory brought him.

But deeper than memory lay some hard core of resistance. It flogged him into effort. Panting, whimpering, he dragged his feet under him, and, clawing at the stone, got to his knees and then to his feet.

He lost his balance and fell down a steep slope into a stream. Pulling himself out of the flood, he huddled beside a tall rock and fought for memory.

It came clear and vivid as a video-print—too clear, too vivid.

He was in a strange building, surrounded by high walls, and he was waiting, waiting for a danger beyond all dangers. It came toward him, unhurried, purposeful. He could feel the beat of power which enveloped it. He must fight. And yet he already knew every move of the coming battle, knew that it was a lost one—

There was the clash of wills, the pouring out of mind force against mind force. There was a sudden leap of confidence at his own strength.

Another mind snaked in to aid his enemy, a devious, evil one which left in its wake an unclean trail. But the two together were not able to force his barrier. He held to the defensive for a while and then struck. Under that blow the evil mind quivered—shrank. But he dared not follow its slight retreat for its partner fought. And now that first mind began to plead—to promise—

"Come in with us. We are of your own kind. Let us unite to rule these stupid cattle—nothing can withstand us then!"

He seemed to listen, but under cover he planned. There

was one very dangerous move he had not yet tried. But it was all that was left him.

So he dropped his barrier, only for an instant. With a purr of triumph the evil fighter surged in and he allowed it. Once it had come too far to retreat he turned on it, surrounded and utterly crushed it. There was a scream which was only mental. And the evil was snuffed out as if it had never existed.

But the other, the one who had beckoned and promised, was still waiting. And at the very moment of his victory it struck, not only with its own force, but with added power it had kept cunningly in reserve. And he had known that this would happen—

He fought, desperately, vainly, knowing that the end was already decided. And he broke, so that that other, exultant, wild with victory, swept in. That which was his will was imprisoned, held in bonds, while his body obeyed the enemy.

Down that blank-walled corridor he marched stiffly, purposefully, a blaster in his hand, his finger on the firing button. But within he was shrieking silently because he knew what he would be compelled to do.

Stabbing flashes of blaster fire cut back and forth across a wide open space. And at the opposite edge of that area was what he had been sent to find—the ranger sled. Against his will he crouched and crept from protection to protection.

He saw men fall and the one who shared this weird journey with him snarled in rage as they went down. The opposition was being overcome—and those who brought them down were his own friends.

One more short rush would take him to the sled. And even as he was wondering why the other who commanded him wanted that so terribly he made the spring. But two who crouched behind its shadow stared up at him in stunned surprise. He knew them—but still his arm and hand were forced down and he fired. The startled croak from the fanged jaws of the nearer rang in his ears as he scrambled into the seat and grabbed at the controls.

With his mind sick and cowering, he only half relaxed under the take-off which slammed him breathless against the padding of the seat. And that other inside his mind set the course, one which sent the slight aircraft spiraling up into the dusky dome, up and up, until it touched a balcony high above the heads of the fighters and another leaped into the sled.

And that other's will goaded them away, speeding out of the hall and away at top speed over the city, heading toward a horizon where a faint rim of gray proclaimed daybreak. Although he was obeying that order he still struggled. It was a noiseless, motionless duel, carried on high above the ancient city, will against will, power against power. And it seemed to Kartr that now the other was not quite so confident—that he was on the defensive, content to hold what he had rather than to attempt to strengthen his control.

How did it end—that fight in the sky? Kartr pillowed his aching head on the stone beside the stream and tried vainly to remember. But that was gone. He could only re-call that he had—had blasted Zinga! That he had brought Cummi safely out of the city. That he had betrayed in his over-confidence and recklessness those who had most rea-son to depend upon him. And realizing all that— He closed his eyes and tried to blank out everything—every-thing!

Exhausted, he must have slept again. For he opened his eyes to be dazed by sun reflected from the water. He was hungry—and that hunger triggered the same instinct of self-preservation which had brought him earlier to the water. His hands were still slow and clumsy but he man-aged to catch a creature which came out from under an overturned stone. And there were others like it.

Toward evening he got to his feet again and stumbled along beside the water. He fell at last and did not try to struggle up. Maybe he dreamed, but he snapped to full wakefulness from a haze in which Zinga had called him. Awake, desolation closed in. Zinga was gone. Almost viciously he dug his hands into his eyes—but he could not wipe from memory the sight of the Zacathan's face as he had gone down under the beam from Kartr's blaster.

It would be best not to try to go on. To just stay here until he went into a world where memory could not follow— He was so tired!

But his body refused to accept that; it was getting up to stagger on. And in time the stream led him out on a wide plain where tall yellow grass tangled about his legs and small nameless things ran squeaking from his path. In time the stream joined a river, broad and shallow so that rocks in some parts of its bed showed dry tops under the sun.

Bluffs began to rise beside the water. He climbed, and slipped, and slid painfully over obstructions and he lost all count of time. But he dared not leave the water, it was too good a source of food and drink.

He was lying full length on a rock by a pool, trying to scoop out one of the water creatures when he started and cried out. Someone—something—had touched his mind —had made contact for an instant! His hands went to his head as if to protect himself from a second calling.

But that came. And he was unable to shut out the alien presence which flooded into him, asking questions—demanding—Cummi! It was Cummi trying to get at him again—to use him—

Kartr threw himself off his perch, skinning his arm raw, and began to run without taking thought. Get away! Away from Cummi—away—!

But the mind followed him and there was no escaping its contact. He found a narrow crevice leading away from

143

the water, half choked with briars and the water-worn drift of storm floods. Unheeding scratches he plunged into the tangle.

It was a very small pocket ending in a hollow under the overhang of the bluff. And into this he crawled blindly, a child taking refuge from a monster of the dark. He curled up, his hands still pressed to his head, trying to blank out his mind, to erect a barrier through which the hunter could not pierce.

At first he was aware only of the desperate pounding of his own heart, and then there was another sound—the swish of an air-borne craft. The contacting mind was closing in. What frightened him so much he could not have explained—unless it was the memory of how the other's dominion had made him kill his own men. What Cummi had done once, he might well do again.

And that fear of his was the other's strongest ally. Fear weakened control. Fear—

With his face buried between his arms, his mouth resting on the gritty soil under the overhang, Kartr stopped fighting the pursuer and tried to subdue his own fear.

Faintly he heard the sound of a shout, the crackling of brush. Cummi was coming down the notch!

The ranger's lips set in a snarl and he inched out of the pocket of earth. His hands chose, almost without help from eye or brain, a jagged rock. He had been tracked like a beast—but this beast would fight! And the Arcturian might not be expecting physical attack, he might well believe his prey to be cowering helplessly, waiting for the master's coming!

Cautiously Kartr pulled himself up so that his back was against the welcome solidity of the gully rocks. His stone weapon was a good one, he thought, balancing it in one hand—just the right size and weight and it had several promising projections.

144

"Kartr!"

The sound he made in answer to that call was the growl of a baited animal.

His name—Cummi daring to use his name! And the Arcturian had even disguised his voice. Clever, clever devil! Illusions—how well that warped brain could create them!

Two figures burst through the brush to face him. The stone dropped from his nerveless fingers.

Was Cummi controlling his sight too? Could the Arcturian make him see this—?

"Kartr!"

He shrank back against the stone. Run—run away—but there was no escape—

"Cummi—?" He almost wanted to believe that this was a trick of the Arcturian's, that he was not honestly seeing the two coming toward him, the smiling two in ranger gray.

"Kartr! We've found you at last!"

They had found him right enough. Why didn't they just draw and blast him where he stood? What were they waiting for?

"Shoot!" He thought he screamed that. But their faces did not change as they came in to get him. And he believed that if they touched him he would not be able to bear it.

"Kartr?" another voice questioned from down the gully.

He jerked at the sound as if a force blade had ripped his flesh.

A third figure in ranger uniform beat through the brush. And at the sight of *his* face the sergeant gave a wild cry. Something burst in Kartr's skull, he was falling down into the dark—a welcoming, sheltering dark where dead men did not walk or greet one smilingly. He hid in that darkness thankfully.

"Kartr?"

The dead called him, but he was safe in the dark and if he did not answer no one could drag him out again to face madness.

"What is the matter with him?" demanded someone.

He lay very quiet in the dark, safe and quiet.

"—have to find out. We must get him back to camp. Look out, Smitt. Use binders on him before you put him aboard, he could twist right over the edge—"

"Kartr!" He was being shaken, prodded. But with infinite effort he locked his lips, made his body limp and heavy. And his stubbornness gave him a defense at last. He was left alone in his dark safety.

Then slowly he became aware of a warmth, a soothing warmth. And, as he had at his first awaking in the wilderness, he lay still and felt his body come back to life. There were hands moving over him, passing over half-healed wounds and leaving behind them a refreshing coolness and ease.

"You mean he is insane?"

Those were words spoken through his dark. He had no desire to see who spoke them.

"No. This is something else. What that devil did to him we can only guess—planted a false memory, perhaps. You saw how he acted when we caught up with him. There are all sorts of tricks you can play—or rather someone without scruples can play—with the mind, your own and others'—when you are a sensitive. In some ways we are far more vulnerable than you who do not try to go beyond human limits—"

"Where's Cummi? I'd like to—" There was a cold and deadly promise in that and something in Kartr leaped to agree with it. And that act of emotion pushed him away from the safety of the dark.

"Wouldn't we all? But we shall—sooner or later!"

A hard edge was pushed against his lips, liquid trickled

146

into his mouth and he was forced to swallow. It burned in his throat and settled into a pleasant fire in his stomach.

"Well, so you have found him?" A new speaker broke through the mists about him.

"Haga Zicti! We have been waiting for you, sir. Maybe you can suggest treatment—"

"So—and what is the matter with the rescued? I see no wounds of importance—"

"The trouble is here." Fingers touched Kartr's forehead. And he shrank away from that touch. It threatened him in some odd fashion.

"That is the way of it, eh? Well, we might have deduced as much. A false memory or—"

He was running away, running through the dark. But that other was behind him, trying to compel him— And, with a moan of desolate pain, Kartr found himself again in the hallway, facing Cummi and the Can-hound, made to relive for the third time that shameful and degrading defeat and murderous attack upon his own comrades.

"So Cummi took him over! He must have used other minds to build up such power—!"

Cummi! There was a hot rage deep inside Kartr, burning through the shame and despair—Cummi— The Arcturian must be faced—faced and conquered. If he did not do that he would never feel clean again. But would he even if he vanquished Cummi? There would remain that moment of horror when he had fired straight into Zinga's astonished face.

"He took over." Was he actually saying those words or were they only ringing in his head. "I killed—killed Zinga—"

"Kartr! Great Space, what *is* he talking about? You killed—!"

"Describe the killing!" And he could not disobey that sharp command.

He began to talk slowly, painfully, and then with a

147

spate of words which seemed to release some healing in their flow. The fight for the sled, the escape, his awaking in the wilderness, he told it all.

"But—that's perfectly crazy! He didn't do that at all!" someone protested "I saw him—so did you, and you! He walked right through the whole fight as if he didn't see any of us—took the sled and went. Maybe he did pick up Cummi as he said—but the rest—it's crazy!"

"False memories," stated the authoritative voice. "Cummi supplied them—guilty ones so that he would want to keep away from us even if Cummi couldn't control him fully. Simple—"

"Simple! But Kartr's a sensitive—he does that sort of thing himself. How could he be taken in—?"

"Just because he is a sensitive he could be that much more vulnerable. Anyway—now that we know what is wrong—"

"You can cure him?"

"We shall try. It may leave some scars. And it will depend upon how adept Cummi has been."

"Cummi!" That was spat out as if the name were an obscene oath.

"Yes, Cummi. If we can turn Kartr's will to meeting— Well, we shall see."

Again a hand was laid on his forehead, soothingly.

"Sleep—you are asleep—sleep—"

And he *was* drowsily content now—it was as if some weight had been shrugged away. He slept.

Waking was as sudden. He was staring up at a sloping roof of entwined branches and leaves—he must be lying in a lean-to such as the rangers built when in temporary camp. There was a cover over his body, one of the blankets of Uzakian spider silk from their packs. He turned his head to see a fire. There was a dankness in the air, a mist or fog dulled the outlines of the trees that ringed in the clearing.

Someone came out of the mist and flung down an armload of wood.

"Zinga!"

"In the flesh and snapping!" returned the Zacathan genially, bringing his jaws together smartly to prove it.

"Then it *was* a false memory—" Kartr drew a deep breath of wonder and infinite relief.

"That was the biggest lie you ever dreamed, my friend. And how do you feel now?"

Kartr stretched luxuriously. "Wonderful. But I have a lot of questions to ask—"

"Which can all be answered later." Zinga went back to the fire and picked up a cup which had been resting on a stone close to the flames. "Suppose you get this inside you first."

Kartr drank. It was hot broth and well flavored. He glanced up with a smile which seemed to stretch muscles that had not been used for a long, long time. "Good. I think I detect Fylh's delicate talent in cooking—"

"Oh, he stirred it up now and then right enough, and added some of his messy leaves. Down every drop of it now—"

But Kartr was still holding the cup and sipping at intervals when another stepped out into the firelight. And the sergeant stopped in mid-gulp to stare. But Zinga was right here, beside him. Then who, in the name of Tarnusian devils, was that?

Zinga followed Kartr's eyes and then grinned. "No. I haven't twinned," he assured the sergeant. "This is Zicti—of Zacan to be sure—but a Hist-techneer, not a ranger."

The other reptile man strolled up to the lean-to. "You are awake then, my young friend?"

"Awake and"—Kartr smiled at them both—"in my right mind again—I think. But it may take some time for

149

me to sort them out—the real and fake memories, I mean—they are rather mixed—"

Zinga shook his head. "Do not work too hard at that sorting until you are stronger. Weak as you are it might set you twirling about like a Tlalt dust demon."

"But where—?"

"Oh, I was a passenger on the *X451,* along with my family. We joined your force yesterday—or rather the rangers found us in the early mornig—"

"What happened in the city after I—er—left?"

Zinga's taloned finger moved with a faint scraping sound along his jaw. "We decided to come away—after the fight was over."

"Hunting for me?"

"Hunting for you, yes, and for a couple of other reasons. Smitt and Dalgre came across a ship the city people built. It brought us this far before it gave out. They are still working on it under the delusion that they may be able to put it back together again if they can just solve a few of its internal mysteries."

"Smitt and Dalgre?"

"Yes, the Patrol withdrew as a unit. It seemed best at the time."

"Hmm." Kartr considered all that statement might imply. There *had* been changes. He was suddenly eager to know how many.

# 12

## *KARTR TAKES THE TRAIL*

Three in the uniform of the Patrol squatted on their heels by the fire. Kartr sat up, his back braced against bedrolls, watching them.

"You never said"—he broke the silence at last—"why you left the city—"

None of the three seemed to wish to meet his gaze. Finally it was Smitt who answered, an almost defiant ring in his tired voice.

"They were grateful to have Cummi and his men removed—"

Kartr continued to wait but that appeared to be all the answer the com-techneer was going to give.

"Big of them," Dalgre added after a long pause, a dry rasp under-running his words.

"They decided," Zinga took up the explanation, "that they did not want to exchange one official ruler out of the past for another—at least the impression they conveyed was that the Patrol had better not plan to take over in Cummi's place. So we weren't welcome—especially the rangers."

"Yes, they made it clear." Smitt was bleakly cold. " 'Now that the war is over, let the troops depart'—the

151

usual civilian attitude. We tended to be a disturbing element as far as they were concerned. So we took one of the city aircraft and left—"

"Jaksan?"

"He went after the jetman who had burned down the Commander. When we found them later they were both dead. We're the last of the Patrol—except for Rolth and Fylh—they're out scouting—"

The three did not enlarge on that story and Kartr accepted their reticence. Perhaps to the city castaways who had tasted Cummi's grab for power the Patrol had become too much a symbol of the old way of things. And so the Patrol had to go, after the ruler who had been rebelled against. But one thing had come of that—there were no longer crewmen or rangers—there was only Patrol—their second exile had cemented tight the bonds of the survivors.

"Ah, our fishing party returns!" Zicti, who had been napping in the warmth of the flames, rolled over and got to his feet to greet the three coming through the screen of the trees. "And what luck did you have, my dears?"

"We put Rolth's blue torch down at the water's edge and the creatures were attracted by its light, so we return heavily laden," the thinner voice of a Zacathan female answered. "This is indeed a very rich world. Zor, show your father the armored creature you found under the rock—"

The shortest of the three ran into the firelight, holding in one hand a kicking thing of many legs and thick claws. Zicti accepted the captive, being careful not to encounter the claws, and examined it critically.

"But how strange! This might almost be a distant cousin of a Poltorian. But it is not intelligent—"

"None of the water dwellers appear to be," agreed his wife. "However, we should be glad of that, for they are excellent eating!"

Kartr had seen few Zacathan women, but his long companionship with Zinga had accustomed him to the difference between human and Zacathan features and he could understand that both Zacita and her young daughter, Zora, would be considered attractive by others of their race. As for young Zor—he was the small boy imp of any species and was enjoying every minute of this wilderness life.

Zacita made a graceful gesture to suggest that the company seat themselves again. Kartr noted that Smitt and Dalgre had been as quick to rise to greet the Zacathan ladies as the others. Their feelings concerning Bemmys had certainly undergone a change.

Kartr awoke early the next morning and lay still for a long moment frowning up at the slant roof of the lean-to. There was something— Then his mouth straightened into a thin hard line. He knew now what it was he had to do and soon. Meanwhile, he crawled out of his bedroll. Above the drowsy quiet of the sleeping camp he could hear the murmur of the river not too far away.

A little unsteadily at first and then firmly as he gained balance he made his way down to its edge. The water was chill enough to bring a gasp out of him as he waded in. Then he lost touch with the sands of its bed and began to swim.

"Ah—the supreme energy and recuperative powers of the young!"

The booming voice was drowned out by a splash. Kartr raised his head just in time to receive a face full of water as Zor passed him at full swimming speed. And Zicti was sliding cautiously down over a flat rock, allowing the stream to engulf him by inches.

The dignified Zacathan blinked in mild benevolence over the wavelets at the ranger sergeant. With two lazy strokes Kartr joined him.

"Pretty primitive, I'm afraid, sir—"

The former hist-techneer of the Galactic University of Zovanta gave a realistic shudder but answered calmly:

"It does one good at times to be shaken out of the comfortable round of civilized life. And we Zacathans are not so physically breakable as you humans. The general idea now held by my family is that this is a most delightful holiday, showing much more imagination on my part than they had believed possible. Zor, for one, has never been so happy—" He grinned as he watched that small scaled body shoot across the current of the stream in pursuit of a water creature.

"But this is not a holiday, sir."

Zicti's large grave eyes met Kartr's. "Yes, there is that to take into consideration. Permanent exile—"

He looked away, over the tumbled rocks, the bluffs beyond the river, the massed greenery of the wilderness. "Well, this is a rich world, and a wide empty one—plenty of room—"

"There is the city, partly in working order," Kartr reminded him.

And in that instant he felt a warmth of reassurance close about him, a mental security he had not known for a long, long time. Zicti was not replying with actual mind speech, but answering the ranger in his own way.

"I believe that those in the city must be left to work out their own destiny," the hist-techneer said at last. "In a manner of thinking that choice is now a retreat. They wish life to remain as it always has been. But that is just what life never does. It goes up—one advances—or it goes down—one retreats. And if one tries to stand still— that is retreat. They are now following the path our whole empire is taking. We have been slowly slipping back for the past century—"

"Decadence?"

"Just so. For example—this spread of dislike for those who are not human. That is increasing. Luckily we Zacathans are sensitives—we are ready to meet situations such as that which ensued after the *X451* set down—"

"What *did* you do then?" asked Kartr, momentarily distracted.

Zicti chuckled. "We landed, too—on a lifeboat. There was a promising tract of wilderness not too far away. Before they got over the surprise of seeing us pop out of the escape port we were safely beyond their reach. But—had we not been able to sense Cummi's attitude—it might have ended differently—

"We came in this direction and established a camp. And I must tell you, sergeant, I was the most amazed being in this solar system when I accidentally contacted Zinga. Another Zacathan here! It was as if I had met a sootacl face to face when I was not wearing a wrist blaster! After we joined forces with your party everything was, of course, satisfactorily explained. They were hunting you—you are very well regarded by your men, Kartr—"

Again that warmth of security and reassurance flooded the sergeant's mind. He colored. "Then, when they found me—"

"Yes, when they found you—well, they loaded you on the lifeboat and brought you here. And your adventure has taught all of us an important lesson—not to underrate an opponent. I would never have believed Cummi capable of such an attack. But, in turn, he was not as strong as he thought himself to be, or you would not have been able to escape from his control after you left the city—"

"But did I?" Kartr's frown was black. "In spite of your therapy I can't remember what happened between leaving the city and waking up alone in the wilderness."

"I believe that you did break free from him," Zicti said soberly. "Which is why I have laid the compulsion on you— But, let us examine the facts—you men of Ylene are six point six on the sensitive scale, are you not?"

155

"Yes. But Arcturians are supposed to be only five point nine—"

"True. But there is always the chance lately that one may be dealing with a change mutant. And this is the proper time in the wave of history for chance mutants to appear. A pity we do not know more of Cummi's background. If he *is* a mutant that would explain a great deal."

"Would you mind," Kartr asked humbly, "telling me just where on the sensitive scale Zacathans place themselves?"

The big eyes twinkled at him. "We have purposely never submitted to classification, young man. It is always best and wisest to keep some secrets—especially when dealing with non-sensitives. But I would rate us somewhere between eight and nine. We have produced several Tel-ones, combination telepaths and teleports, and more only a step or two below that point, during the past three generations. So I am sure that while such mutation is on the increase among my people, it must be working in other races also."

"Mutants!" Kartr repeated and he shivered. "I was on Kablo when Pertavar started the Mutant Rebellion—"

"Then you know what can come of such an upcurve in mutant births. There are good and bad results from all changes. Tell me, when you were a small child, were you aware of being a sensitive?"

Kartr shook his head. "No. In fact I was never aware of my powers until I entered the ranger cadet school. Then an instructor discovered my gift and I was given special training."

"You were a latent sensitive. Ylene was a frontier planet, its people too close to barbarism to know their full strength. Ah—to have such a vigorous world thrown away! The foul sins of war! It is just because things such as the destruction of Ylene are happening too often now

156

that I am convinced our civilization is nearing its end. Now in this camp we are a queer mixture." He pulled himself out of the water and applied a towel with vigor. "Zor, it is time to come!" he called after his son.

"Yes, we are a strange mixture—a collection of odds and ends of the empire. You and Rolth, Smitt and Dalgre, are human, but you are all of different races and widely separated stock. Fylh, Zinga and my family are non-human. Those back in the city are human and highly civilized. And, who knows yet, there may also be natives in this world. One might almost believe that Some One or Something was about to conduct an experiment here." He chuckled and sniffed the air. "Ah, food, and I am indeed empty! Shall we go to see what lies in the cooking pots?"

But before they came up to the fire Zicti touched Kartr's arm.

"There is only one thought I wish to leave with you, my boy. I know little of your race—you may not be a mystic, although most sensitives tend to look beyond the flesh and seek the spirit—and you may have no religious beliefs. But if we *have* been chosen to work out some purpose here, it is up to us to prove worthy of being so selected!"

"I agree," Kartr returned shortly but he knew that the other recognized his sincerity.

The Zacathan nodded. "Fine, fine. I am going to enjoy my declining years. And to think I have been given this just when I thought that life was totally devoid of excitement. My dear"—he raised his voice to address Zacita—"the aroma of that stew is delightful. My hunger increases with every step I draw nearer to the fire!"

But Kartr spooned up the soup mechanically. It was very well for Zicti to paint the future in such bold strokes. A hist-techneer by his training was always taught to look at the whole situation, not to study details. Now ranger instruction worked in just the opposite fashion, it was the small details which mattered most, the careful study of a new planet, the long hours of patient spying upon strange peoples or animals, the rebuilding by speculation from a few bricks of a whole vanished civilization. And here and now they were faced with a detail which he and he alone must handle.

He must render Cummi harmless!

That was the thought which had held over from sleep that morning, had been part of his dreams, and was now crystallized into a driving urge. Living or dead—he must and would find the Arcturian. If Joyd Cummi were still alive he was a menace to all of them.

Queer—Kartr shook his head as if to clear it—he was so haunted by that thought. Cummi was a danger, and Cummi was *his* business. Luckily the Arcturian was no trained explorer-woodsman, he must leave a trail so plain it would be child's play for a ranger to follow. They had been together when they left the city. Somewhere that night they had parted company. Had Cummi pushed him off the sled in the dark, intending the fall to kill him? If that were so it would be a much more difficult task to locate the Arcturian—he would leave no footprints on clouds. The thing for Kartr to do was to return to that ledge where he had first gained consciousness.

"That's ten—maybe fifteen miles north—"

The sergeant started to hear the words come from Zinga's thin lips—picked out of his own thoughts.

"And—Kartr—you do not go alone, not on that trail!"

He stiffened. But Zinga must know his protest without his putting it into words.

"That job is mine," the sergeant returned, his teeth set hard.

"Granted. But still I say you do not take such a trail alone. We have the lifeboat—it will cover ground with time-saving speed. And with it we can better prospect for any traces of Cummi's passing."

158

That was good common sense, but it was no sweeter to swallow because it was logical. Kartr would rather have left camp alone and on his two feet. It burned inside him that Cummi was his alone, and that he would not feel whole and well again until he had fronted the Arcturian and won.

"Take one more day of rest," Zinga advised, "and then, I promise, we shall go. This matter of Cummi—it is one of importance."

"Others might not think so. He is alone in a wilderness he can know very little about. The wilds may already have done our job for us."

"But he is Cummi, and so will continue to linger as a threat until we are sure of him. Did Zicti tell you that he believes him a change mutant? Remember Pertavar and what that one was able to do. And Cummi is not going to win next time you face him!"

Kartr smiled at the Zacathan, a smile which was hardly more than ten per cent humor. "D'you know, my friend, there I think you are right! And this time I do not believe that I am being too confident—the mistake I made before. He has no Can-hound—and surely no other brains to tap!"

"Very well." Zinga arose. "Now let me go and pick Dalgre's store of mechanical knowledge. It might be wise to know just how much ranging power the lifeboat unit has left."

They took off the next morning and no one asked questions although Kartr was sure they all knew his mission. The lifeboat did not have the springy lift of the sled and its pace was slower. Zinga, at the controls, held it steady over the winding reaches of the river until they found the stream which had served to guide Kartr's wanderings.

From time to time the Zacathan glanced anxiously at the heavy clouds bulging over the horizon. Storm was indicated and they had best take shelter when the wind which was driving those clouds struck. To be tossed about the sky in a light-weight lifeboat was no experience to be desired.

"Anything below look familiar?"

"Yes. I'm sure I crossed this open field. I remember pushing through the tall grass. And those trees ahead are promising. Think we'd better land in their shelter?"

Zinga measured the cloud spread again. "I'd like more to reach that ledge where you came to. Flame bats! it's getting dark. Wish I had Rolth's night eyes."

It was darkening fast and the rising wind swept under the boat so that it lurched as it might on pounding sea waves. Kartr clung to the edge of his seat, his nails biting into its cover.

"Wait!" He got the word out at the risk of a bitten tongue as the lifeboat bucked. Through the dusk he had caught a glimpse of a recent rock slide down the side of a hill beside the stream. "This looks like where I fell!"

They were already past the point but Zinga circled back, as Kartr squinted through the storm dusk and tried to imagine how that same section would look to a man lying flat on the ledge near the top of the rise.

The aircraft snapped out of the circle and veered suddenly to the right, across the crest of the hill. Kartr's protest was forgotten as he sighted what had drawn Zinga's attention. The top of a tree had been shorn off, the newly splintered wood of the trunk gleaming whitely. With the pressure of expert fingers on the controls the Zacathan set the lifeboat down on the slope of the rise, a piece of maneuvering which might have at another time brought honest praise from the sergeant. But now Kartr was too intent upon what might lie just beyond the broken tree.

He found a mass of crushed branches and the remains of the sled. No one, not even a master mech-techneer, could ever reassemble what lay there now. The wreckage was jammed almost bow down in tight wrappings of withered leaves and broken wood and it was empty.

Zinga sniffed deeply as his torch revealed the bareness of that crumpled seat.

"No blood even. The question is—were either or both of you aboard when she hit?"

Kartr shook his head, a little awed by the completeness of the crack-up.

"I don't think either of us could have been. Maybe he threw me out and—"

"Yes—and if you fought back that could have made him lose control so this would happen. But then where is Cummi—or his remains. No mess at all—something would remain if he had been collected by a wandering meat eater—"

"He could have jumped just before she hit," suggested the sergeant. "If he had an anti-grav on his belt he could have made it on such a short fall without smashing himself."

"So we look for a few tracks now?" Zinga's long jaw jutted out as he glanced up at the sky. "Rain is going to spoil that—"

For the clouds were emptying their weight of water at last. Together the rangers stumbled through a beating downpour to the lea of a rock outcrop which gave a faint hint of shelter. The trees might have kept off more of that smothering blast but, Kartr decided as he saw branches whiplash under the wind, that might be more dangerous an asylum than the corner where they huddled gasping, the rain stinging their skin and finding its way through every crevice of their tunics and breeches.

"It can't keep on like this forever—there isn't that much water," Kartr said and then realized that the drum of rain drowned out any but a parade ground pitch of voice.

He sneezed and shivered and thought bitterly that

161

Zinga was going to be proved right. This deluge would mask any trail Cummi might have left hereabouts.

Then, in an instant, he snapped erect and felt Zinga's answering jerk. The Zacathan was as startled as he had been.

They had caught a faint, very faint plea for help. From Cummi? Somehow he believed not. But it had come from a human—or rather from an intelligent mind. Someone or something which was alive, and reasoning, was in trouble. The sergeant turned slowly, trying to center the source. The pain and terror in that plea must be answered!

## CUMMI'S KINGDOM

"Due North—" Zinga's gutturals reached him, and the Zacathan's keener perception was right.

"Can the lifeboat ride this?" Kartr's own experience with small air craft had been limited to those of the Patrol and the stability of their exploring sleds was proved—they had been designed for rough going under strange weather conditions. But the machine they had to use now did not arouse any confidence in him.

Zinga shrugged. "Well, it isn't the sled. But the force of the wind is lessening and we certainly can't start out on foot—"

They sprinted through the wall of falling water. And a moment later gained the cramped cabin of the lifeboat. It was a relief to be out of the pounding rain. But, even as they settled into their seats, the light craft rocked under them. Get this up into the full force of the wind—they would be riding a leaf whirled around in a vortex—!

But, with that thought in both their minds, neither hesitated. Zinga started the propeller beams and Kartr sent out a mind probe, trying to touch the one who had asked for their help.

They were lucky in some things, the dusk of the storm

clouds was clearing. And Zinga had been correct, the wind was dying. The light plane bucked, swerved, dipped and soared as the Zacathan fought at the controls to hold her on course. But they were air-borne and high enough above the tree tops to escape the fate of the wrecked sled.

"Should circle—?" Zinga thought instead of spoke.

"Enough fuel?" Kartr asked in answer to that as he leaned forward to read the gage on the instrument board.

"You're right—can't afford that," Zinga agreed. "A quarter of a tal of bucking these winds and we'll be walking anyway—"

Kartr did not try to translate "tal" into his own terms of measurement. He had a suggestion to make.

"Pick out some good landmark ahead and set us down—"

"Then we take to our feet? It might work. It will—if this deluge slackens. And there is your landmark—agreed? Put us in the middle of that—"

"That" lay about a mile before them, a wide circle of bare and blackened ground covered with the charred stumps of trees among which the thin green heads of saplings were beginning to show. Sometime not too far in the past this section had been burnt over. Zinga brought them down where the stumps were fewer.

And just as they left the lifeboat that plea for help reached them again, the terror in it plainer. Kartr caught something else. They were not the only living things to answer that call. There was a hunter on the trail ahead, a four-footed hunter, hungry—one who had not fed that day or the night before.

The slot of an old game trail led across the burnt land. Years of pressing hooves and pads had worn it so deep that it could be followed by touch as well as by sight. Kartr's boots slipped into it easily and he trotted on through the slackening rain toward a sharp rise of bare rock. The rock wall which had once kept the fire from advancing was broken in one place by a narrow gap through which the game trail led. And then it went down slope into the heart of a real forest.

Not too far ahead was the hunter, very close to its prey. Kartr caught the mind of the one who was trapped. It was human—but not Cummi. A stranger, hurt, alone, and very much afraid. A different mind—

Now the hunter knew it was being followed. It hesitated—and Kartr heard a cry which was hardly more than a moan. There was a screen of bushes through which he beat his way and then he stood looking down at broken tree limbs and at a small, pitifully thin body pinned to the ground by one shattered branch. A distorted face was turned up to him—and he saw that the captive was no straggler from the city.

Kartr threw himself down in the soft muck and tried to lift the weight of the limb. But he could not shift it far enough for the other to escape. And now the hunter waited—just beyond a neighboring clump of bushes.

"Yahhhhh—" That rising, horrible bellow was the battle cry of a Zacathan warrior. A blaster cracked above Kartr's head.

The tawny furred body had been met in mid-spring by a searing shaft of flame. And the power of the beam bore it back, already terribly dead, into the very nest of leaves from which it had just sprung. A thick stench of singed hair and flesh curled about them.

Kartr went back to work. He was scooping the soft earth from under the branch when a shriek of pure, unreasoning terror whipped him around.

The captive's face was a mask of naked fear, distorted out of human shape.

But there was nothing there to fear—the giant cat was dead. Only Zinga stood there, slipping his blaster back into its holster.

Only Zinga—but it was the Zacathan who aroused that fear!

Kartr did not need to give warning, the other ranger had sensed what was happening and disappeared, melting back into the bushes instantly. Kartr saw the captive was limp now, eyes closed—unconscious! Well, if he would stay that way for a while it would simplify the task.

As silently as he had vanished Zinga came back and together they worked until they had that slim body free and straightened out between them on the ground. Kartr's hands made quick and skilled examination.

"No bones broken. The worst damage is this." There was a deep and ugly gash across the ribs where a fold of the stranger's flesh had been pinned by a sharp stub.

The body was thin, outlines of ribs showed beneath the sun-browned skin. And the stranger was small and slight—very small to be full grown or close to that, as Kartr judged the boy to be. His head was covered with a tangled, mud-and-briar-filled mass of yellow hair and there were downy sproutings along the lines of his jaw and across his upper lip. His torn garments consisted of a sleeveless, open jerkin made of the hide of some animal and a pair of leggings of the same material, while there were queer bag-like coverings on his feet.

"Very primitive—a native?" Zinga wondered.

"Or a survivor of another wreck—"

The Zacathan bit at one talon. "Might be. But then—"

"Yes—if the stranger was the survivor of another galactic shipwreck why his terror at the sight of you?"

The Zacathans were widely known, and they did not arouse fear—they had never been raiders. But—Kartr studied his companion objectively for the first time—suppose one had never seen a Zacathan before? Suppose one's world was only inhabited by beings more or less like one's self? Then the first glimpse of those pointed, fanged jaws, of that scaled skin, of the frill depending about a hairless head and neck—yes, it would be enough to frighten a primitive mind.

Zinga nodded; he had followed that reasoning. Now he had an answer ready.

"I'll go back to the lifeboat and keep out of sight. You can try to discover where he came from and all the rest. If you move him, I'll follow. Natives here! What if Cummi finds them?"

But Kartr did not need that implied warning. "Get going now— I think he's coming around!"

Eyelids flickered. The eyes they had shielded were light blue, almost faded. First there was terror mirrored in them, but when they saw only Kartr's human features the fear went and a sort of wary curiosity took its place. The sergeant probed lightly and found what he had suspicioned. This was no survivor of a space shipwreck, or, if the lad was descended from galactic rovers, their landing on this forsaken world was many generations back.

To make entirely sure of that Kartr asked his first question in the speech so common to all travelers of the stellar routes.

"Who are you?"

The boy was puzzled and his surprise deepened into fear once more. He was not accustomed to hearing a strange tongue, apparently, and galactic speech meant nothing to him. Kartr sighed and returned to the easiest methods of communication. He jabbed a thumb at himself.

"Kartr—" he said slowly and distinctly.

The wariness remained, but the curiosity was stronger. And after a moment of hesitation the boy repeated the ranger's gesture and said:

"Ord."

Ord. That might be the native term for man, but Kartr thought it more likely a personal designation. Again, and with infinite caution, the sergeant tried mind contact. He expected some shrinking, fear— But, to his surprise and interest, the boy appeared familiar with such an exchange. Yet—surely—he was not a sensitive! Kartr went deeper and knew that the stranger was not.

Which meant only one thing—he had had in the past some dealings with a sensitive—enough not to fear the mind touch. Cummi! The sergeant's own signal went out to Zinga. The Zacathan was in the lifeboat ready and waiting.

Kartr turned to Ord. Making the boy comfortable on a bed of boughs under the drooping branches of a neighboring tree where the rain could not drench them so completely, he went to work. Sometime later, with mind touch and a fast-growing vocabulary, he learned that Ord was one of a tribe who lived a roving life in the wilderness. Any mention of the city sent him into shivering evasion—it was in some manner taboo. Those "shining places" had once been the homes of the "sky gods."

"But now the gods return—" Ord was continuing. Kartr's attention snapped to "alert."

"The gods return?"

"Even so. One has come to us, seeking out our clan— that we may serve him as is right—"

"What is the appearance of this sky god?" asked the sergeant, keeping his voice carefully casual as if it mattered very little.

"He is like unto you. But—" Ord's eyes widened— "but then are you also of the sky gods!" And he made a gesture with crossed fingers pointed at the ranger.

Kartr took the plunge. "After your way of speaking— yes, I come out of the sky. And I am trying to find the god who is now among your people, Ord."

The boy moved uncomfortably, inching away from the sergeant. His hand fell on his bandaged side and he looked up with the old wary suspicion.

"He said that there were those who might come hunting him—night demons and doers of evil. And"—terror colored his voice again—"when first you came upon me I thought I saw with you such a one—a demon!" His voice slid up scale until it was almost a scream.

"Do you see him now, Ord? I, alone, am here with you. And you say that I look like the sky god who is with your people—"

"You must be truly a god—or a demon. You killed the silent hunter with fire. But if the god who came to us is your friend, why did he say that those who came after him were his enemies?"

"The ways of the gods," Kartr answered loftily, "are not always the ways of men. Had I been a demon, Ord, would I have brought you out from under that tree, bandaged your hurt, and treated you well? I think that a doer of evil would not have done that for you."

The other responded to this simple logic almost eagerly. "That is right. And when you come with me to the clan we shall have a great feast and later we shall go together to the Meeting Place of the Gods where you can be as you were in the very ancient days—"

"I want very much to go with you to your clan, Ord. How may we reach them?"

The boy's hand pressed his injured side and he frowned. "It lies one day's travel away—does the camp. I will not be able to walk swiftly—"

"We shall manage, Ord. Now this 'Meeting Place of the Gods'—that is where your people live?"

"No—it is much farther away. Ten days of travel from here—maybe more. We go once a year, all the clans together, and there is trading and warriors are raised up at the Man Fire, and the maidens make their choices of mates. There is fine singing and the Dance of Spears—" His words trailed off.

Kartr smoothed the matted hair back from the boy's eyes.

"Now you will sleep," he ordered. The pale blue eyes closed and the boy's breathing came even and unhurried. Kartr waited for a few minutes and then slipped into the fringe of trees where seconds later Zinga joined him.

"This 'sky god' he speaks of must be Cummi—" the sergeant began.

"Cummi, yes, and with him at large time is of importance. This Ord is a member of a primitive, superstitious culture—just the type Cummi could wish for—"

"He can start a fire in such tinder which would spread with ease," Kartr agreed. "We've got to get to him!"

His fingernails drummed on his belt. "We'll have to take the boy," he continued. "And he says that the camp is at least a day's journey away. I can't carry him that distance—"

"No. We'll take the lifeboat."

"But, Zinga, he thinks you are a demon. He couldn't be dragged aboard that with you in it—"

"No? But there is going to be no trouble. Use your wits, Kartr. You are a sensitive but you have no idea even yet of how much power you have to draw on at will. Ord will see and hear just what I want him to when we go and he will guide us to just the right spot, too. But we shall not land at his camp—I cannot control any number of minds—especially where Cummi has been tampering. So you will carry him in to his people and he will have no memory of the flight or of there being a second ranger."

It went just as Zinga had promised. Ord seemed but half awake, lying between them in dreamy content. He answered the Zacathan's questions readily. The visibility was better than it had been all day and they were flying out of the rain.

"Smoke!" Kartr pointed to the right.

"That must be their campsite. Now for a landing place—not too far away. You take him in—"

Ten minutes later Kartr grunted as he paused, the boy's

limp body in his arms. He was on the edge of an open park-like expanse in which were set up, in no particular order, a cluster of skin tents. He could sense some twenty individuals within range of mind touch. But not Cummi.

"Ord!"

A girl was running toward the ranger, long braids of the same yellow hair as the boy's swinging over her shoulders.

"Ord?" She stopped short, staring with a hint of terror at the sergeant.

To his relief the boy roused at her cry and turned his head.

"Quetta!"

There were others coming from the tents now. Three men, hardly taller than the boy, moved warily along, their hands not far from the hafts of the long knives at their belts. Their cheeks and chins were covered with thick mats of hair—they were furred almost like animals.

"What you do?" The demand came from the tallest of the three.

"Your boy—hurt—I bring him—" Kartr shaped the unfamiliar words slowly and as clearly as he could.

"Father—this is a sky god—he seeks his brother—" Ord added.

"The sky god is away. He hunts."

Kartr gave silent thanks for the chance to learn the ground before Cummi's return. "I will wait—"

They did not dispute that. Ord was taken from him and established on a pile of furs in the largest of the tents. And the ranger was given a mat by the fire and offered a steaming bowl of stew. He ate hungrily but it was not appetizing stuff.

"How long ago did—did the sky god leave?" he asked at last.

Wulf, the hairy chieftain and Ord's father, squinted and sucked upon a tightly rolled stick of dried leaves which he had lit with a blazing splinter and moved contentedly between his bearded lips, puffing out a gray, acrid smoke.

"With the first light. He is very clever. With his magic he holds fast the beasts until the young men can spear them. We feast in plenty since he came to us. He will go to the Meeting Place of the Gods and there call upon his people and they shall come to us. Our maidens shall marry with them and we shall be great and rule this land—"

"Your people have lived here always?"

"Yes. This land is ours. There was a time of burning fire and the gods departed into the sky—then we were left behind. But we knew that they would come again and bring a good life with them. And so it has come to pass. First came Koomee"—he had trouble with the name— "now you are here. There will be others—as the old ones promised."

He puffed silently for a moment or two and then added, "Koomee has enemies. He said that the demons fear that he may make us great again."

Kartr nodded. He gave every appearance of listening closely to what the chieftain was saying, but he was listening with more than ears alone. They were expert woodsmen, these natives. For the past five minutes they had been creeping into position in the dark behind him. They planned a sudden rush—a neat enough idea—it might have worked with a non-sensitive caught in the trap. As it was he could turn and put hand on every one of them. And he must make some move before that rush came.

"You are a great and clever chieftain, Wulf. And you have many strong warriors, but why do they lurk in the dark like frightened children? Why does he with a split lip crouch there"—the sergeant pointed to his left— "and the one with the two knives there?" His hand moved from side pocket to the fire as Wulf's head jerked around. A tongue of greenish flame shot up to bring light to the faces of the men who had believed themselves completely hidden.

There was a wild animal howl of fear as they threw themselves back out of that betraying light. They scattered. But to give full credit to the chieftain's courage he did not move. Only the roll of leaves dropped from his mouth to singe the hide legging on his right knee.

"If I *were* a demon," Kartr continued in his ordinary voice, "those would now be dead men, for I could have slain them as they hid. But I have no hatred for you or your people in my heart, Wulf."

"You are Koomee's enemy," returned the other flatly.

"Has Cummi said so? Or do you only guess that? Let us wait until he returns—"

"He has returned." The chieftain did not turn his head but there was a subtle alteration in his voice, a quickening of intelligence in his eyes as if another personality now inhabited the squat body.

Kartr got to his feet. But he did not draw his blaster. He could only use that weapon for a last defense. Surely the Arcturian wouldn't hurl these poor fools at him—!

"That I shall believe when I face him. Gods do not fight from behind others—"

"So say the noble Patrol! The fearless rangers!" Wulf's lips twisted as he shaped words entirely alien to his own tongue. "You are still bound by those outmoded codes? The worse for you. But I am glad you have come back to me, Sergeant Kartr, you are a better tool than these brainless woodsrunners."

And before Wulf had half finished that speech a bolt of mental force struck Kartr. If Cummi had not betrayed himself by words he might have had a better chance. But the ranger was armed and prepared. And into him flowed Zinga's support, so that he stood smiling faintly in the firelight as he parried and thrust in the silent motionless duel.

Cummi did not try heavy assaults, instead he used quick rapier stings of attack which one must guard against constantly. But Kartr's confidence grew. And he was doing all the work, he realized with mounting exultation—Zinga was only in watchful support. Let Cummi be a change mutant of unknown powers, he was going to meet his match now in a frontier barbarian from a vanquished planet. The ranger had a second's flicker of new knowledge—Ylene had been burnt off because an Arcturian had realized the threat of that world.

His confidence grew. Perhaps Ylene had been the check upon the growing Arcturian ambition. Very well, a man from Ylene was about to avenge both his people and his world!

# 14

## PLAGUE

But that confidence was to be suddenly shaken. The pressure exerted by Cummi stopped as quickly as if some force blade had cut it. And in place of that darting attack there was a confused boiling of unrelated thoughts and impressions. Was that to lure him from behind his block, to set him up for some more subtle attack? But Kartr remained wary, ready to meet what came—and it came with a wild blast of desperation as if the Arcturian must win at once.

That ebbed and still the sergeant was on guard, believing that the other had withdrawn to gather his forces for another assault. And by thinking that he almost died.

For the attack which came was not mental but physical—a lance of blaster fire.

With a choked cry of pain Kartr dropped. He lay flaccid in the glow of the flames.

The chieftain shook his head and stared almost stupidly at the limp body of the ranger. He was still in the process of getting to his feet when another came out of the shadows and approached the fire, a gleaming blaster in his hand.

"Got—got him!" There was an odd hesitation in those words of triumph. And before he reached the body the newcomer stopped and half raised his hand to his head.

Then his face twisted and he cried out. The blaster fell to the ground, bounced, and landed close to the body of his victim. And a second later he, too, had crumpled up.

Kartr raised himself. His hand went to his left shoulder. The vlis hide jerkin had taken some of the force of the blast, and it had not been well aimed. He had a nasty burn, but he was still alive, scooping up Cummi's blaster as he got to his feet.

That blaster—why had Cummi tried to burn him down? The sergeant was sure that the Arcturian relied on mental power—the weapon was entirely out of character—Cummi was too civilized, too self-confident. And how in the world had he been able to knock the Arcturian out so easily just a minute ago? Why—Cummi had reacted to his bolt as if he had had no mind blocks up at all!

As the ranger bent over him Cummi stirred and moaned faintly. The Arcturian's breath came in painful gasps, his chest laboring as if he were fighting hard for every lungful of air. But that was not natural—what *was* wrong with the man?

"Koomee? What does—?"

Wulf hovered timidly by the two. Kartr shook his head.

"Turn him over," he ordered briefly.

The chieftain obeyed gingerly, as if he dreaded touching the man on the ground. Kartr went down on one knee, setting his teeth against the sharp twinge of pain that motion cost him. In the firelight the Arcturian's sharp features were plain to see, his mouth was open and he was gasping. There was a faint, dark shadow pinching in about his beaked nose and about his lips—Kartr stiffened.

"Emphire fever!" he broke out though Wulf could not understand.

It was a common enough disease, he had had a bout with it once himself. The answer was galdine. But before the medicos had discovered that drug emphire had been serious all right. A man who caught it strangled to death because muscles locked against breathing. Galdine! But where could one find galdine here? Did they carry it in their packs of ranger equipment? He tried to remember if it were included. It might not be—their immunity shots were supposed to leave them free from the necessity of carrying such supplies.

In the meantime Cummi was going to die unless he could get air. And he, Kartr, couldn't apply artificial respiration with a blast-burned shoulder.

"You"—he turned to Wulf—"put your hands here. Then push hard and let go, like this—one, two, one, two—"

With visible reluctance the chieftain obeyed orders. Kartr contacted Zinga.

"Cc," came the calm response. "Will try for galdine in camp if you can hold on. Give me two hours—maybe three—"

Kartr bit hard on his lower lip; little hot waves of pain spread from the burn.

"Get going!" he flashed back.

Wulf glowered at him from under the tangle of his thick hair.

"Why must I do this to Koomee?"

"If you fail to do it he will die."

For a moment the rhythm ceased as the chieftain looked at the ranger in open surprise.

"But there is no wound upon him. And he is a sky god—one of those of all knowledge. Have you laid a spell upon him—being his enemy?"

"There is no spell." Hurriedly Kartr discarded two possible explanations and gave a third which this clansman might not only understand but accept. "Cummi has swallowed certain demons which cannot be seen. They do not wish to come forth, but they must be forced to do so—or

177

they will slay him as surely as if your knife had torn him open—"

Wulf considered this and went back to his task. The manpower—and womanpower—of the camp ringed them in. And, as Wulf began to tire, Kartr arbitrarily chose the nearest and strongest of the men and set him to work in the chieftain's place. The sergeant watched Cummi's face narrowly. He could not be sure but he was almost certain that some of the strain was passing.

It might be that the first attack would be over before Zinga returned. Emphire came in cycles, he recalled. If the first disastrous paralysis of the disease did not kill, there was a period of relief before the second attack began. For that second crisis only galdine was the answer. If not treated with it the patient generally succumbed. The fever, which had faded in four generations to light attacks of mild discomfort, had once been a plague which had devastated whole planets.

Yes, Cummi was definitely breathing easier. At a sign from the ranger the man now working over the Arcturian stopped, but the Vice-Lord continued to draw shallow breaths. Kartr touched the dank skin of the sick man's face; the characteristic cold sweat was beading on forehead and upper lip.

"Bring robes to cover him," he told them.

Wulf pulled at his sleeve. "Are the demons out?"

"They have withdrawn; they may yet return."

A woman squirmed by the line of men and tossed a tanned skin in the general direction of Cummi. But she came no closer to draw it over the unconscious man. Kartr pulled it awkwardly into place himself. The natives were edging away. Wulf had retreated to the other side of the fire where he hovered nervously as if in two minds about whether to follow his people into the tight group of whisperers by the tents.

Two hours, Zinga had said, maybe three. And perhaps

no galdine after all. Kartr didn't like to see the natives gathering that way, to hear the whispers hissing in the dark. They couldn't start any trouble without his knowledge. But he was one man against twenty or more of them. He had two blasters—which he could only use as a very last resort. The years-long conditioning of the rangers would not permit him to fire until it was absolutely necessary in order to save his life.

"You—"

That weak thread of voice came from beside him. Cummi was awake.

"What—?" The Arcturian began a question.

Kartr answered with one word: "Emphire."

"Beaten—by—by a virus!" There was self-contempt in that. "Galdine?"

"Maybe. I have sent someone to see if it is among our supplies."

"So? Then there *were* two of you!" Cummi's voice was gaining strength. "But you are alone now—"

"I am alone."

The Arcturian's eyes closed wearily. He was holding a complete mind block. Perhaps behind it he was planning. But emphire affected the mental powers as well as the muscles. He could do little to start trouble now.

"You are going to have difficulties with the clan, you know." He was continuing in a conversational tone, a sort of malicious amusement just below the surface. "I've had time to indoctrinate them pretty thoroughly. They are not going to take kindly to my collapse—they'll believe that you've tried to murder me."

Kartr did not answer and his silence appeared to sting Cummi to another effort.

"You won't win this bout, Ranger, any more than you won the last. If I die you'll go down under their knives and spears—a fitting end for a barbarian."

The sergeant shrugged although that motion almost

wrung a cry of pain from him. Cummi's half-open eyes narrowed and a grin drew back his lips in an animal snarl.

"So I did mark you! Well, that will make you easier meat for Wulf and his men when the time comes."

"You have it arranged very neatly, I suppose." Kartr dared to yawn. He might not be able to read what was going on behind the Arcturian's block, but he could guess how he himself would answer such an impasse and he gave Cummi credit for devising something as easy. "I will be taken care of and then you will lay an ambush for whoever comes with the galdine. It will be simpler to get it from a dead man."

But Cummi's eyes were closed again and he gave no sign that the other might have scored. Kartr looked to Wulf. The chieftain was sitting cross-legged again, staring into the fire. Was Cummi busy now making mind contact with that hunched figure? The sergeant sighed. During the past few days he had discovered that there were vast unexplored possibilities tied up with this gift of his. Why, the adept who had schooled him had known practically nothing—he knew that after meeting with Zicti, discovering communication with Zinga. If he had *their* ability now he might well be able to intercept any orders or suggestions the Arcturian was trying to plant in Wulf's mind. He had no idea of the extent of Cummi's power—if he were a change mutant, anything was possible.

The rest of the clan were still bunched in the dark by the tents. But they were squatting down, there was no immediate danger of attack. He had only to be alert and ready—

Time passed leadenly. Now and again someone crept up to feed the fire. Wulf drowsed and awakened with a jerk of the head. To all appearances Cummi either slept or was unconscious. But Kartr stayed on guard. Fortunately the pain in his shoulder would not let him rest.

At last the sound he had been straining to hear

came—the faint swish of the lifeboat's air passage. He drew a deep breath of relief and straightened. Then he glanced down. Cummi's eyes were open, dark holes of evil malevolence. What was the Arcturian going to try?

Wulf stirred and Kartr's hand reached for the blaster Cummi had dropped. The chieftain arose stiffly to his feet. Three more men came out of the shadows to join him.

"Kartr!" That mental call was imperative and it came from Zicti not Zinga. "There is no galdine!"

Even as the message reached the ranger Cummi uncoiled, his legs flailing out in a move which might have brought Kartr down had he not sprung backward at the same instant. The Arcturian was crazy if he thought he could ever surprise a sensitive. But by his maneuver the Vice-Lord had been able to get to his hands and knees.

This was it! Kartr lurched to the left, keeping the fire between him and the clansmen who were moving to come up to him. They had their knives out. And he couldn't turn his blaster on the poor fools, he couldn't!

He lashed a kick at Cummi, who, reflexes weakened by the fever, could not dodge the blow. As the Arcturian sprawled flat on his face, the ranger hurdled his body and began to back toward the woods in the general direction of the hidden aircraft.

Seconds later he heard a welcome voice behind him.

"I have them covered, Kartr—"

"Cummi controls them—"

"Cc. I've got him, too. Fall back to the trees, Zicti is waiting for us." Rolth spoke calmly as he stepped out of the shadows to stand shoulder to shoulder with the sergeant.

Cummi caught at Wulf as the chieftain passed him. Using the native as a support he pulled himself up on his feet.

"So you don't have galdine," he spat at them. His face

was no longer malevolent. It was twisted and white with pure fear.

"I may be a dead man," he went on softly, "but I still have time to finish you, too." He released Wulf suddenly and pushed him at the rangers. "Kill—!" he screamed.

"We'll do what we can for you—" Kartr said slowly.

The Arcturian was holding himself erect with an effort which was draining the last resources of his strength. "Still living by the code, fool! I shall live to see your blood—barbarian!"

"Ahhhhhhhh!" The scream was shrill and it bit rawly at the nerves. It could only have been torn from a woman's throat.

Wulf and his men half turned just as a second scream broke. There was a frenzied gabble of words which Kartr did not catch. But Zicti's thought translated for them.

"One of this tribe—a maiden—has fallen ill. They believe that the demons of Cummi have entered into her—"

Wulf had gone to the source of the screaming; now he came back into the firelight walking heavily.

"The demons"—he spoke directly to the Arcturian— "are in Quetta. If you are truly a sky god—bring them forth."

Cummi swayed, conquering the weakness of his body by sheer power of will.

"It is their doing." He pointed to the rangers. "Ask them."

But Wulf's attention did not waver.

"Koomee is a sky god, he has sworn it. These have not sworn it. Koomee brought the devils hither in his body. They are the devils of Koomee, not the devils of my people. Now let Cummi summon them forth out of the body of my daughter!"

Cummi's ravaged face, gaunt and hollowed, was a mask of pain in the flickering light. His black eyes held on the rangers.

"Galdine." Kartr saw the Arcturian's lips form the word. Then slowly, as if he were fighting to the last, he lost control and toppled forward into the trampled dirt and ashes on the very edge of the fire.

Wulf stooped and twisted his fingers in the Arcturian's cropped hair, fumbling for a hold, and then he jerked up the head. But Cummi had lost consciousness. And, before either of the horrified rangers could move, the chieftain drew his knife in a quick stroke across the stretched throat of the Vice-Lord.

"Here is an open door for the devils to enter," he remarked, "and also much blood for them to drink. May they speedily find it." He wiped the knife on Cummi's tunic. "Sometimes it takes very much blood to satisfy the thirst of a strong demon," he ended as he looked up at the rangers.

Rolth's blaster was ready but Kartr shook his head. Together they backed into the darkness under the trees.

"They will follow—" suggested the Faltharian.

"Not yet," came Zicti's reassurance. "I think that they are still a little daunted by their chieftain's act. After all, it is not every day that one slays a god—or ex-god. Now, let us make haste to the lifeboat."

It was morning again and there was a sun bright and hot across Kartr's knees but his thoughts were dull and gray.

"We couldn't do anything to help them." Smitt was making his report. "If we had had the galdine—maybe— if they would let us near them. But we have tried during these last three days. When Dalgre and I went there two hours ago one of them crawled out just to throw a knife at us. Most of them must be already dead." He spread out his hands in a gesture of defeat. "I do not think any will be alive by nightfall."

"Twenty people—maybe more—murdered. It was murder," Kartr returned bleakly.

"We don't catch it," Dalgre wondered.

"Immunity shots—and the Zacathans have never come down with emphire. But this is the way it used to hit— when it was a plague. It hasn't been like this for years—"

"We've had galdine. And we've known emphire a long time, remember. It struck us just after the Sirius worlds were explored. Through generations," Rolth pointed out, "we may have built up some natural immunity to it, also. Man does, by natural selection. But how do we know how many other germs we may carry with us—harmless to us but devastating to this world. The best thing we can do from now on is to stay away from the natives."

"And that move may not be altogether altruistic," added Zinga. "Suppose they have bred some pleasant little viruses of their own. Let us pray that our immunity shots continue to work."

"It is a tragedy, but one we can do nothing to end." Zicti pulled off his traveling cloak and let the sun beat warmly on his shoulders. "From now on we shall keep away from these people. I gather that they are not a numerous race—?"

"I believe not," answered Kartr. "From the little I was able to learn there are only a few small family clans—but they unite once a year at—"

"The Meeting Place of the Gods, yes, that is a most interesting point. These 'gods' who departed into the sky— who were they, some galactic colony later withdrawn? That would account for the city left in order to wait a return. Pardon me, gentlemen, I am being swept away again by my own subject." The hist-techneer smiled.

"But there was no space ship landing field near the city," protested Dalgre.

"That was only one city. There may be others," Fylh pointed out. "Suppose they had only one or two space ports on the whole planet. That could be true of a colonial outpost."

184

"The Meeting Place of the Gods," mused Zicti. "What does that suggest?"

"We've got to go there!" Dalgre sat up eagerly. "The city machinery, what I saw of it, was in an amazing state of preservation. If we find a space port we might even find a ship we can use!"

A ship to use. Kartr frowned. And then he could only be surprised at the instant protest those words had sparked in him. Didn't he want to leave this world?

Zacita and her daughter came out of the makeshift tent that was their own domain and joined the group by the fire. Kartr noted with an inner tickle of amusement how quick Zinga was to heap up the grass intended for seating.

"You have news of importance?" Zacita asked.

"There may be an ancient space port near here. The native boy told Kartr of a 'Meeting Place of the Gods' which suggests possibilities," replied her husband.

"So—" Zacita considered that. But Kartr caught a fleeting impressing that she was not altogether pleased with that news. Why? A Zacathan lady of the highest rank—for the gold forehead paint she wore proclaimed her an Issitti, one of the fabulously wealthy and noble Seven Families—certainly would rejoice at the chance to return to galactic civilization as quickly as possible.

"Techneer Dalgre believes that if we find one of the old ships we might be able to activate it again—since the machinery in the city was in such an excellent state of preservation. They used a city form of aircraft to come here, remember—"

"I hope that any space ship we might discover would last longer than that did," Dalgre struck in ruefully. "It did bring us this far but then it went to pieces."

"An important point to consider." Kartr met Zacita's eyes and it was almost as if he read in them some subtle encouragement. "I have no desire to blast off in a ship which will go powerless after we hit deep space. I can

185

think of many more effective and less painful ways of committing suicide—"

"But we can visit this Meeting Place of the Gods." Dalgre was almost pleading.

"I would say yes, if we can keep free of the natives. It is time for their annual pilgrimage there. And we can't mingle with them. Cummi infected and killed that clan just as truly as if he had taken a disruptor to their camp! We can't be walking death to a whole nation!"

"Very true," Zicti agreed. "Let us do this—send out a scouting party to make mind contact with some clan bound for this assembly. But our men must keep out of sight. The natives thus discovered will serve us as unconscious guides. Once contact is established we can follow with our supplies— Will the lifeboat be of any more service?"

"It can go twenty—maybe twenty-five miles." Dalgre answered that with authority.

"Well, walking is good for the figure," Zicti continued good-humoredly. "What do you think, Sergeant Kartr?"

"You have the best solution," Kartr returned.

Zinga got up, crooking a taloned finger in Rolth's direction. "Let us go out by night—owl eyes here can watch and I can think us into contact. Should we find what we seek, you shall speedily know of it."

# 15

## THE MEETING PLACE
## OF THE GODS

Before midnight they received the message they had been waiting for, Zinga and Rolth had found a clan of natives camped for the night and had made sure that they were en route to the Meeting Place of the Gods. In the late afternoon of the next day the rangers abandoned their own camp and set out on the trail blazed by their unknowing guides.

On the eighth morning both Kartr and the Zacathans caught the warning of a multitude gathered not far ahead—they must be approaching their goal. And, picking a well-sheltered and secluded thicket, they made camp, sleeping uneasily by turns until nightfall when Zinga, Kartr and Rolth set out to learn the general lay of the land before them.

It was not the lights of a city which lit a glow in the northern sky to beckon them, but the rising flames of at least a hundred campfires. The three rangers moved gingerly about the rim of the wide, shallow cup which held the clan rendezvous, avoiding any near contact with the few stragglers still coming in.

"This *is* a rocket port!"

"How can you be sure?" demanded Kartr, striving to see what had made Rolth declare that with such firmness.

"The ground—all over this depression—it has been blasted time and time again by take-off back-flares! But it's old—no new scars showing."

"All right. So we've located an old space port." Zinga sounded irritated, almost disappointed. "But a port isn't a ship. See any of those, bright eyes?"

"No," Rolth returned calmly. "But there is a building on the other side—there. See—that fire lights it just a little—"

Kartr, now that his attention had been directed, sighted it, an expanse of massive blocks only barely perceptible in the poor light.

"It's large—"

Rolth cupped his hands around his eyes to cut some of the fire glare. "Let's have the visibility lenses, Kartr." And when he used those he added with a faint trace of excitement:

"It's huge—bigger than anything we saw in the city! And—did you ever visit Central City?"

Kartr laughed bitterly. "I saw a visigraph of it. Do you think we outer barbarians ever came so close to the fount of all knowledge as to see it in reality?"

"And what has Central City got to do with this?" Zinga wanted to know. "Were you ever there yourself?"

"No. But one can get a pretty good idea of the place from the visigraphs. And that building over there is an exact duplicate of the Place of Free Planets—or I'll eat it stone by stone!"

"What!" Kartr snatched the lenses out of his companion's hands. But, although the fires and the figures of the natives moving about them leaped up to meet his eyes, the building beyond remained only a shadowy blurred shape shrouded in the night.

"But that is impossible!" Zinga cried out almost triumphantly. "Even the newly hatched know that the Place of Free Planets is archaic, designed by architects who lived so far in the past we don't even know their names or home worlds. And it has never been copied!"

"Except that it has—right here," Rolth returned stubbornly. "I tell you, there is something queer about this world. Those tales you heard, Kartr, of the 'gods' who took to space—that city left waiting, ready for its owners to return, this place where the natives have a tradition that they must gather at regular intervals to await such a homecoming—it all adds up—if we only knew how to add—"

"Yes," agreed Kartr, "there is some mystery here, a bigger one maybe than we have ever tried to solve before—in spite of our system ranging—"

"Mysteries!" Zinga scoffed. "And now, my friends, we had better withdraw in a hurry unless you wish to be trampled by a select party from below—"

But Kartr had received the same sense warning and was already creeping on his hands and knees back from the rim of the ancient space port.

"If we made a wide circle to the west," Rolth pointed out, "we might be able to come out behind that building and see more of it."

So the Faltharian wanted to see more of it. Kartr shared his impatience. A solitary building which resembled the sacred Place of Free Planets! He must get to the bottom of the mystery; he had to! A world not included on even the most ancient routing tapes which he had seen—in a solar system so near the rim of the galaxy that it had been overlooked—or forgotten—centuries before he was born. Yet here beside an age-old space port stood a replica of the oldest and most revered public building ever built by human beings! He must find out why—and who—and what—

During the next few hours they made the western circle

Rolth had suggested, and when, just before dawn, they were joined by the other rangers and Patrolmen, they were behind the building. Kartr's eyes were sticky with sleep but excitement would not let him go back to their camp. He had to see what Rolth had described.

They moved from cover to cover, at last crawling snakewise to reach a point from which they could see clearly.

"Rolth was right!" Dalgre's voice rose to a squeak in his amazement as he looked down at the white mass. "My father was stationed at Headquarters one year—we lived in Central City. I tell you that's the Place of Free Planets down there!"

Kartr's hand pushed him flat. "All right, we'll take your word for it. But keep your voice and your head down. Those men below are trained hunters—they could easily spot you."

"But how did it get here?" Dalgre turned an honestly bewildered face to the sergeant.

"Maybe"—Kartr brought out the thought which had been born in him during the night—"this came first—"

"Came first!" Smitt wriggled up and screwed the lenses tight to his eyes. "Came first—but how?"

"You mean it could be that old?" breathed Rolth.

"You've the lenses, Smitt. Take a good look at the edge of the roof and the steps leading up to the portico—"

"Yes," the com-techneer agreed a moment later. "Erosion—that place is very old."

"Older than the city even—" he added. "Unless being set out alone in the open had hastened decay. I'd like to have a closer look—"

"Wouldn't we all?" Zinga interrupted him. "How long do you suppose our friends down there are going to sit around?"

"Some days at least. We'll just have to button up our

curiosity until they do leave," Kartr answered. "It'll probably keep us busy to just elude parties coming in and going out. We had better stay some distance away from now on."

Smitt uttered a slight groan of protest and Kartr could sympathize with him. To be so near and yet have to refrain from covering that last quarter mile which kept them from the mystery was enough to irritate anyone. But they did withdraw and there was no argument over the wisdom of keeping aloof from the natives.

Their account of the building intrigued Zicti and the next morning he calmly appropriated the services of Zinga, saying:

"Since I am unfortunately not acquainted with the proper methods of lurking, crawling, and dodging, I shall require the aid of an expert to teach this old one new tricks. Alas, even when removed, perhaps permanently, from my lecture halls, I cannot suppress my desire to collect knowledge. The customs of these natives are certainly of great interest and with your permission, Sergeant, we shall lurk and crawl to watch them—"

Kartr grinned. "With my permission, or without it, sir. Who am I to interfere with the gathering of knowledge? Though—"

"Though"—Zicti caught his thought smoothly—"it may be the first time in many years that one of my rank has gathered source material personally in the field? Well, perhaps that is one of the ills of our civilization. A little personal attention can often stop leaking seams, and a fact learned from a fragment of one culture can be applied to salve the ills of another."

Kartr ran his hands through his hair. "They are a good people—primitive—but we could help them. I wish—"

"If we only had the medical skill and learning we could mingle with them in safety. Or *you* could. Whether they would ever accept a Bemmy"—Zicti stabbed a talon at his own arched breast—"is another question. Among primitives, what is the general attitude toward the unknown? They fear it."

"Yes—that poor boy thought that Zinga was a demon," Kartr replied reluctantly. "But in time—when they learned that we meant them no harm—"

Zicti shook his head regretfully. "What a pity that we do not have a medico among us. That is one of the few limitations of our present situation which bothers me."

"You are ready to march, Haga Zicti?" Zinga came up to them, bowing his head and addressing the elder Zacathan with one of the Four Titles of Respect, which confirmed Kartr's suspicions that the hist-techneer was a noble on his own world.

"Coming, my boy, coming. There is one thing which I and my household may thank the First Mother for," he added, "and that is that we have such companions in misfortune!"

Kartr, warm with pleasure, watched the two Zacathans out of sight. He realized that Zicti, much as he withheld from giving any opinion until asked, or from intruding upon the ranger councils, was a leader. Even Smitt and Dalgre, for all their inborn suspicion not only of unhumans but also of sensitives, had fallen under the spell of the urbane charm and serene good nature of the hist-techneer and his family. The Patrolmen fetched and carried cheerfully and readily for Zacita and Zora, and preserved a lordly big-brother-plagued-by-small-tag-along attitude toward Zor. Just as the difference between ranger and crewman had vanished, so had that between human and Bemmy.

"And what are you thinking of when you stand there smiling at nothing at all?" Fylh dropped a bundle of firewood and stretched. "You should come and haul in some of these logs—if you have nothing better to do."

"I was thinking that there have been a lot of changes," began the sergeant.

But for once he found Fylh as intuitive as Zinga. "No more Bemmys, no more crew and rangers, you mean? It just happened—somehow." He sat down on the woodpile. "It may be that when we got out of the city they"—he jerked his head in the direction Smitt and Dalgre had taken a few minutes previously—"had to make a choice, once and for all. They made it, and they aren't looking back. Now they don't think about differences—any more than you and Rolth ever did—"

"We were almost Bemmy ourselves, Rolth with his night sight, and I a sensitive. And I was a barbarian into the bargain. Those two are both inner-system men, more conventional in their conditioning. We must give them credit for conquering some heavy prejudices."

"They just started to use their brains." Fylh's crest lifted. He raised his face to the sky and poured out a liquid run of notes, so pure and heart tearing a melody that Kartr held his breath in wonder. Was this Fylh's form of happy release from emotion?

Then came the birds, wheeling and fluttering. Kartr stiffened into statue stillness, afraid to break the spell. As Fylh's carol rose, died, and rose again, more and more of the flyers gathered, with flashes of red feathers, blue, yellow, white, green. They hopped before the Trystian's feet, perched on his shoulders, his arms, circled about his head.

Kartr had seen Fylh entice winged things to him before but never just this way. It appeared to his bewildered eyes that the whole campsite was a maze of fluttering wings and rainbow feathers.

The trills of song died away and the birds arose, a flock of color. Three times they circled Fylh, hiding his head and shoulders from sight with the tapestry of tints they wove in flight. Then they were gone—up into the morning. Kartr could not yet move, his eyes remained fixed on

193

Fylh. For the Trystian was on his feet, his arms out-stretched, straining upward as if he would have followed the others up and out. And for the first time, dimly, the sergeant sensed what longings must be born in Fylh's people since they had lost their wings. Had that loss been good—should they have traded wings for intelligence? Did Fylh wonder about that?

Someone beside him sighed and he glanced around. The three Zacathans, Zacita, Zora, and Zor, stood there. Then the boy stooped to pick up a brilliant red feather and the spell was broken. Fylh dropped his arms, his feather crest folded neatly down upon his head. He was again a ranger of the Patrol and not a purveyor of winged magic.

"So many different kinds—" That was Zacita, with her usual tact. "I would not have dreamed that these trees give harborage to so many. Yes, Zor, that is indeed an unusual color for a sky creature. But every world has its own wonders."

Fylh joined the Zacathan boy who was smoothing the scarlet feather delicately between two talons. "If you wish," he said with a friendliness he had not often dis-played before, "I can also show you those who fly by night—"

Zor's yellow lips stretched in a wide smile. "Tonight, please! And can you bring them here in the same way?"

"If you remain quiet and do not alarm them. They are more timid than those who live by the sun. There is a giant white one who skims through the dark like a Corrob mist ghost—"

Zor gave an exaggerated shiver. "This," he announced loudly, "is the best holiday we have ever had. I hope that it is never going to end—never!"

The eyes of the four adults met above his head. And Kartr knew they shared the same thought. This exile would probably never end for them. But—did any of

194

them care? Kartr wanted to ask—but he couldn't—not just yet.

The rangers spent the day overhauling their equipment and making minor repairs. Clothing was a problem—unless they followed the example of the natives and took animal skins to cover them. Kartr speculated about the coming cold season. Should they tramp south to escape its rigor? For the sake of the Zacathans perhaps they should. He knew that exposure to extremes of cold rendered the reptile people torpid until they lapsed into complete hibernation.

They spied upon the natives, going out in pairs to do so, turning in all information to Zicti who compiled it as if he fully intended to give a documented lecture on the subject.

"There are several different physical types among them," he commented one evening when Fylh and Smitt, who had drawn that day's watch, had given their report. "Your yellow-haired, white-skinned people, Kartr, are only one. Now Fylh has seen this clan of very dark-skinned, black-haired men—"

"By their light clothing and strange equipment they are from a warmer country," added the Trystian.

"Odd. Such dissimilar races on the same world. But that is a humanoid characteristic, I believe," continued the hist-techneer. "I should have had more grounding in humanoid physiology."

"But they are all very primitive. That is what I can't understand." Smitt wore a puzzled frown as he spooned up the last of his stew. "That city was built—and left all ready to run again—by men who were in a high state of technological advancement. Yet all the natives we have discovered so far live in tents made of animal hide, wear skins on their backs, and are afraid of the city. And I'll swear that that pottery I saw them trading today was made out of rough clay by hand!"

"We don't understand that any better than you do, my boy," answered Zicti. "We never shall unless we can penetrate the fog of their history. Some powerful memory—or threat—has kept them out of the city. If they ever possessed any technical skill they forgot it long ago—maybe by deliberately suppressing such knowledge because it was sacred to the 'gods,' perhaps because of a general drop in a certain type of intelligence—there could be many explanations."

"Could they be the remains of a slave population, left behind when their masters emigrated?" ventured Rolth.

"That, too, would be an answer. But slavery does not usually accompany a highly mechanized civilization. The slaves would be machine tenders—and the city people had robots which would serve them better in that capacity."

"It seems to me," began Fylh, "that on this world there was once a decision to be made. And some men made it one way, and some another. Some went out"—his claws indicated the sky—"while others chose to remain—to live close to the earth and allow little to come between them and the wilds—"

Kartr straightened. That—that seemed right! Men choosing between the stars and the earth! Yes, it could have happened just like that. Maybe because he, himself, was a barbarian born on a frontier world where man had not long taken to space, he could see the truth in that. And perhaps because Fylh's people had made just such a choice long ago and sometimes regretted it, the Trystian had been the first to sense the answer to the riddle here.

"Decadence—degeneracy—" broke in Smitt.

But Zacita shook her head. "If one lives by machines, by the quest for power, for movement, yes. But perhaps to these it was only a moving on to what they thought a better way of life."

A moving on! Kartr's mind fastened on that eagerly.

196

Maybe the time had come for his own people to make a choice which would either guide them utterly away from old paths—or would set them falling back—

Time continued to drag for the watchers until the last of the natives departed. They even waited another five hours after the last small clan left, making sure that there would be no chance of being sighted by lingerers. And then, in the middle of an afternoon, they came down the slope at last, picking their way through the debris of the campsite and around still smoldering fires.

At the foot of the stairs which led to the portico of the building they left their packs and bundles. There were twelve broad steps, scored and pitted by winds of time, with the tracks of hide sandals outlined in dried mud where the natives had wandered in and out. Up these steps they climbed and passed through lines of towering pillars into the interior.

It would have been dark inside but the builders had roofed the center section with a transparent material so that they could almost believe they still stood in the open.

Slowly, still in a compact group, they came down an aisle into the very middle of the huge hall. Around them on three sides were sections of seats, divided by narrow aisles, each ending at the floor level in one massive chair on the back of which was carved, in such high relief that time had not worn it away, a symbol. On the fourth side of the chamber was a dais supporting three more of the high-backed chairs of state, the center one raised another step above the other two.

"Some type of legislative building, do you think?" asked Zicti. "The presiding officer would sit there." He pointed to the dais.

But Kartr's torch beam fastened on the sign carved on the nearest of the side chairs. As he read it he stood incredulous. Then he flashed the light to illumine the marking on the next seat and the next. He began to run, reading the symbols he knew—knew so well!

"Deneb, Sirius, Rigel, Capella, Procyon." He did not realize it, but his voice was rising to a shout as if he were calling a roll—calling such a roll as had not sounded in that chamber for four thousand years or more. "Betelgeuse, Aldebaran, Pollux—"

"Regulus." Smitt was answering him from the other side of the hall, the same wild excitement in his voice. "Spica, Vega, Arcturus, Altair, Antares—"

Now Rolth and Dalgre began to understand in turn.

"Fomalhaut, Alphard, Castor, Algol—"

They added star to star, system to system, in that roll call. In the end they met before the dais. And they fell silent while Kartr, with a reverence and awe he had never known before, raised his torch to give more light to the last of those symbols. That bright one which should gleam in this place was there!

"Terra of Sol." He read it aloud and the three words seemed to echo more loudly down the hall than any of the shouted names of the kindred stars. "Terra of Sol—man's beginning!"

## 16

## TERRA CALLING

"I don't believe it." Smitt's voice sounded thin; his attention was fixed on that high seat and the incredible sign it bore. "This can't be the Hall of Leave-Taking. That was in Alpha Centauri—"

"Was it?" asked Kartr. "Our legends placed it there. But legends are not always the truth."

"And out there"—Dalgre pointed toward the doorway without turning his head from the dais—"is the Field of Flight!"

"How long—?" Rolth's question dwindled off into silence, but his words continued to echo down the hall.

Kartr wheeled to face those rows of chairs and the section of seats each one headed. There—why, right there had sat the commanders, and behind them crews and colonists! And so they must have gathered, shipful after shipful for years—maybe centuries. Gathered, spoke together for the last time, received their last orders and instructions—then went out to the field and the waiting ships and blasted off into the unknown—never to return. Some—a few—had won through to their goals. They, Smitt, Dalgre, Rolth and he, were living proof of that. Others—others had reached an end in the cold of outer space or on planets which could not support human life. How long had it gone on, that gathering, that leave-taking? With no return. Long enough to drain Terra's veins of life—until only those were left who were temperamentally unfitted to try for the stars? Was that the answer to the riddle of this half-and-half world?

"No return—" Rolth had picked that out of his thoughts somehow. "No return. So the cities died and even the memory of why this exists is gone. Terra!"

"But *we* remember," Kartr answered softly. "For we have made the full circle. The green—that is the green of Terra's hills. It has been a legend, an ancient song, a dim folk memory, but it has always been ours, going with us from world to world across the galaxy. For *we* are the sons of Terra—inner system, outer system, barbarian and civilized—we are all the sons of Terra!"

"And now," Smitt observed with wistful simplicity, "we have come home."

It was a home which bore no resemblance to the dark mountains and chill valleys of Rolth's half-frozen Falthar, to his own tall forests and stone cities now forever dust, to the highly civilized planets which had been the birthplaces of Smitt and Dalgre. It was a planet of wilderness and dead cities, of primitive natives and forgotten powers. But it was Terra and, as different as their races might be today, they were all originally of the stock which had walked this earth.

Once more he surveyed that assembly of empty seats. Almost he could people it. But those he summoned to sit there could not be the ones who had once done so. The men of Terra had been gone too long—were scattered too far—

He walked slowly down the center of the hall. The Zacathans and Fylh had drawn apart. They must have watched with amazement the actions of the humans. Now Kartr tried to explain.

"This is Terra—"

But Zicti knew what that meant. "The ancient home of your species! But what an amazing discovery!"

What else he might have added was drowned out in a shout which drew all their attention to the dais again. Dalgre stood at the left of it beckoning to them. Rolth and Smitt had disappeared. In a body they hurried to join Dalgre.

The new discovery was behind the dais, hidden by a tall partition—and it covered most of the wall. A giant screen of some dark glass on which pin points of light made patterns.

Below it was a table top of which was inlaid with a paneling of switches and buttons. Smitt crouched on the bench before it, his face intent.

"A communication device?" asked Kartr.

"Either that or some kind of a course plotter," Dalgre answered. Smitt merely grunted impatiently.

"Could it still be in working order?" Zacita marveled.

Dalgre shook his head. "We can't tell yet. The city functioned again after they pulled the right switches. But this"—he indicated the giant star map and the intricate controls on the table—"will have to be studied before *we* can push the right levers. Why, we don't understand any of their wiring methods—"

The techneer, any techneer, might possibly put the machine into working order again. But, Kartr knew, such a feat was totally beyond the rangers. He studied the star map slowly, identifying the points he could recognize. Yes, here was the galaxy as it appeared from this ancient planet close to its rim. He noted the brilliance of Vega, moved on to Alpha Centauri and the others. Had this board once plotted the course on which man went out to those far-off suns and the worlds they nourished?

It was growing darker as the evening closed down. But even as the light faded from overhead, a soft glow outlined the star map and illumined the table—although the rest of the hall remained shrouded with shadows.

Kartr moved. "Shall we camp outside or return to the hills?" he asked Zicti.

"I see no reason for returning," the Zacathan replied. "If all the natives have withdrawn, as they apparently have, surely there can be no objection to our staying—"

Behind him Zinga laughed and pointed a talon at Smitt. "If you think that you can drag him away from here even by force, you are sadly in error, Sergeant."

Which, of course, was true. The com-techneer, confronted by a mysterious device in his own field, refused to leave even for food, preferring to gulp down a cup of water and chew on a piece of tough meat absently while his eyes were busy with the marvels before him.

They chose to drag their bedrolls into the hall when the full night fell, putting out their cooking fire and lying closely together below the empty seats of the vanished colonists.

"There are"—Zicti's voice boomed through the emptiness—"no ghosts in this place. Those who gathered here once were already voyaging on in spirit, even as they sat here, eager to be gone. They have left nothing of themselves behind."

"In a way," Rolth agreed, "that was also true of the city. It was—"

"Discarded." Kartr produced the right word as the Faltharian hesitated. "Discarded as might be a garment grown too small for its wearer. But you are right, sir, we shall meet no ghosts here. Unless Smitt can awaken some with his tinkering. Is he going to stay there all night?"

"Naturally," Zinga replied. "And let us hope that he will *not* raise any voices out of the past—even out of your human past, friend. I have an odd desire to spend this night in slumber."

Kartr awakened twice during the night. And by the

faint glow which crept around the edges of the partition he saw that Smitt's bedroll was still unoccupied. The com-techneer must be hypnotized by his discovery. But there was a limit to everything. So, at his second awakening, Kartr pulled himself out of the warmth of his bed with an impatient sigh, shivered in the chill, and padded on bare feet across the cold stone. Either Smitt would come willingly or he would be dragged to bed now.

The com-techneer was still on the seat, his head thrown back, his gaze fixed on the star map. In the reflection of the light his eyes appeared sunken and there were dark shadows like bruises along his cheek bones.

Kartr followed the direction of the other's set stare. He saw what held Smitt fascinated, blinked, and gave a gasp.

There was a red dot on the black glass surface, a dot which moved in a steady curve.

"What is it—"

Smitt replied without taking his eyes from the traveling dot.

"I'm not sure—I'm not sure!" He passed his hands across his face. "You *do* see it, too?"

"I see a red dot moving. But what is it?"

"Well, I've guessed—"

And Kartr knew the nature of that guess. A ship— moving through space—headed in their general direction!

"Coming here?"

"It's on a course—but—how can we tell? Look!"

Another dot had sprung into being on the screen. But this moved with a purpose. It was on the track of the first, a hunter on the trail. Kartr pushed down beside Smitt on the bench. His heart was thumping so that he could feel the sullen beat of blood in his temples. It was very important—that flight and pursuit—somewhere within him he knew that—so important he feared to watch.

The first dot was moving in a series of zigzags now.

"Evasive action." Smitt mouthed the words. He had served on a battle cruiser, Smitt knew.

"What kind of ships are they?"

"If I understood this"—Smitt swept his hand over the controls before him—"maybe I could answer that. Wait—!"

The first dot engaged in a complicated maneuver which had no meaning as far as the sergeant could see but which flipped it back on a level with its pursuer.

"That's a Patrol ship! It's offered battle—but why—"

They were even, those two dots. And then—a third appeared on the board! It was slightly larger and moved more slowly, avoiding the two which would shortly be locked in combat. And, in making the arc to avoid the fight, it headed straight toward Sol's system.

"Covering action," Smitt translated. "The Patrol is covering for this other ship! A suicide mission, I think. Look—their battle screens are up now!"

A faint, very faint orange haze encircled the two dots near the outer verge of Sol's system. Kartr had never been in space action, but he had heard enough tales, seen enough visigraphs, to be able to create in his mind a picture of the struggle now beginning. The larger dot had no part in the struggle. Instead it crept at its snail's pace on and on, away from the dead-locked fighters.

Pressure—pressure of screen against screen. And when one of those screens failed—flaming and instant death! That was a Patrol ship out there holding the enemy at bay while a defenseless prey escaped.

"If I could only read this!" Smitt smashed his fists against the edge of the table.

On the board a tiny bubble of light blazed suddenly to light.

"Set off by the ship coming this way?"

Smitt nodded. "Could be." He leaned forward with quick decision and pressed his finger on the button set under that pinprick of light. There followed sound—a vast roar as of rushing winds. They stared at the map almost deafened. And then through the roar came the chatter of something else, a sharp clicking which formed a pattern. Smitt jumped to his feet.

"Patrol summons, Patrol summons—TARZ—TARZ—"

Kartr's hand reached for a blaster he was not wearing. The old call to action for the Service! He heard amazed cries behind him. The others were up, crowding around the partition to see and hear what was happening.

The beat of the summons echoed hollowly through the building. It might go on until the end of that battle or until there was some answer. But no answer came. The haze about the dots thickened until they were completely hidden in it and each spot was a stationary fire.

"Top pitch—!" That was Dalgre breathing the words down Kartr's back. "Reaching overload fast. They can't take that much longer—they can't!"

"Tar—"

One spot swept from orange to yellow—to incandescent white. It was an instant of splendor and then it was gone. They blinked blinded eyes and looked again. But there was nothing—nothing at all of the two fiery spots. The dark glass of the screen where they had been was as bare and cold as the wastes of outer space it represented.

"Both—out!" Dalgre was the first to speak. "Overload and it blasted them both. One ship took the other with it."

"But the third—it is still intact—" Zicti pointed out.

That was true. The battle had wiped out two ships, but the third dot still moved—the one which the Patrol ship had died to save. It was on course—toward Sol and Terra!

The clicking sound changed, made another series of coded calls. Smitt listened and read them aloud for his companions.

"Patrol—auxiliary—personnel ship—2210—calling nearest Patrol ship or station. Come in, please—come in. Survivors of Patrol Base CC4—calling nearest Patrol ship or station—off known courses—need guide call—come in, please—"

"Survivors of Patrol Base CC4," Rolth repeated. "But that was a Ranger Station! What in the name of Space—!"

"Pirate raid, maybe—" suggested Zinga.

"Pirates don't tangle with the Patrol—" began Dalgre.

"You mean—pirates didn't! We've been out of circulation and off the maps for some time. A coalition of pirate forces can do a lot of damage," Zinga observed.

"Note also," Zicti added to that, "this ship now flies from the more populated sections of the galaxy. It heads out toward the unknown which it would not do if there were not some barrier between it and more familiar routes."

"Personnel survivor ship—families of Patrolmen." Dalgre was visibly shaken. "Why, the base must be utterly gone!"

The clicking of the code still filled the musty air of the hall. And on the map the dot moved, on the board before Smitt the tiny bulb still blazed. Then, as suddenly, it snapped off and a second went on in turn in the block next to it. Kartr glanced from that new light to the screen. Yes, the dot was appreciably closer to the system of Sol.

Smitt's fingers hovered over the board. He licked his lips as if his mouth was dry.

"Is there any chance of guiding her in here?" Kartr asked the question he knew was tormenting the other.

"I don't know—" Smitt snarled like a tortured animal.

His finger went down and pressed the button below the second light. And then he jumped back, as did Kartr, for out of the edge of the table sprang a thin black stalk end-

206

ing in a round bulb. The com-techneer laughed almost wildly and clutched at the thing.

Then he began to speak into it, not in code but in the common tongue of Control Center.

"Terra calling! Terra calling! Terra calling!"

They were frozen, silent, listening to the chatter of the code filling the air. Kartr sagged. It hadn't worked after all. And then came a break in the ship's broadcast. He had forgotten about the time lag.

"Terra calling." Smitt was cool, calm again. To that statement he began to add a series of code words and clicks. Three times he repeated the message and then leaned back to await reply.

Again the wait seemed too long—tearing at their ragged nerves. But at last an answer came. Smitt translated it for them all.

"Do not entirely understand. But think can ride in on message beam—keep talking if you have no signal. What—where is Terra?"

So they talked. First Smitt, until his voice was but a husky whisper issuing from a raw throat, and then Kartr, using ordinary speech and the old formula, Terra calling—then Dalgre and Rolth—

There was sunshine lighting the space around them and then it grew dark again and still they crouched in turn on the bench before the sky map and talked. And the red dot crept on, now on a straight course for Terra. It was when it had drawn almost even with the outermost planet of Sol's system that Zor pointed out to the half-dazed Kartr on duty, the newcomer. Another dot—already past the point where the battle had been fought—and on a line after the personnel ship! Enemy or friend?

Kartr shook Zor's shoulder and pushed him toward the outer hall with the message to bring Smitt. The com-techneer, rubbing sleep-heavy eyes, half reeled in. But when Kartr showed him the dot he was thoroughly awake. He shoved the sergeant away from the microphone and took over with a sharp question in code.

After lagging minutes it was answered:

"Undoubtedly enemy ship. Pirate signals have been picked up during last quarter hour—"

To Kartr's sick eyes the enemy ship was darting across space. It was now a race, a race in which the Patrol ship might already be the loser. And, even as he thought that, there was a flash of light on the control board. The enemy was now within hailing distance. Smitt turned a grim face to him.

"Get one of the Zacathans and Fylh. If they can talk in their own language it will be better than using control speech or the code as a guide. There are few Bemmys in pirate crews. All the ship needs is a steady sound to center her finder on—"

But he spoke his last words to the empty air. Kartr was already on his way to rout out the others. Seconds later Zinga slipped into Smitt's place, hooked his talons around the stem of the phone and unloosed a series of hissed sounds which certainly bore no resemblance to human speech. When he tired, Fylh was ready and then twittering and fluting broke across space to talk the ship in. But ever relentlessly behind it came that other dot, seeming to leap across great expanses of space as if such stretches were nothing.

Zora brought in a canteen of water and they all drank feverishly. They ate after a fashion, too, of whatever was thrust into their hands, unknowing and untasting.

The Patrol ship passed more planets. Then a third light snapped on the board. Zor came running in.

"There is a big light—reaching into the sky!" he shouted shrilly.

Kartr jumped to his feet to see that for himself when a sound of ship's code stopped him.

"Pulse beam picked up. We can ride it in. If we still have time—"

Zinga let go of the phone and as one they hurried out into the open. Zor was right. From the end of the roof directly over the control table a beam of light speared into the evening sky.

"How did that—?" Kartr began.

"Who knows?" Dalgre replied. "They were master techneers in their day. That must pulse strongly enough to be picked up by a ship approaching this planet within a certain distance. At least we can now stop talking."

In the end they drifted back to the map—to watch the ship and its pursuer. The gap between those two was narrowing—too quickly. A last light flashed on the control board—it was warning red.

"Ship's entered the atmosphere," Smitt guessed. "Get everybody inside here. It may not land on the field and the rocket wash will be brutal—"

So they waited inside the ancient Hall of Leave-Taking and they heard rather than saw a ship land on a field which had not felt the bite of rocket fire for at least a thousand years. But it was a good landing.

Smitt remained at the board. "That other is still coming—" His warning rang out to hasten the others.

Still coming! They might lose even now, Kartr thought, as he watched the exit bridge swing out from the side of the rusty old tub perched on its landing fins in the field. All the enemy would have to do would be to hover and blast them with rockets. He wouldn't have to land, but when he pulled out again he would leave nothing behind but a blackened and lifeless waste.

If they could get the refugees into the hall they might have a chance to survive that—a very thin one. The sergeant ran to the edge of the smoking landing area and waved at the figure who had appeared on the bridge.

"Get your people off and into the hall!" he shouted. "The pirate's coming and he can try for a burn-off!"

He saw the jerk of an assenting nod and heard orders. The passengers filed down the bridge at the double quick. They were mostly women, some carrying or leading children. The rangers and the Zacathans stood ready to act as guides. Kartr half hauled, half carried the strangers to the precarious safety of the old building. Then when the flow of refugees ceased he hurried back to the bridge.

"All out?"

"All out," the officer replied. "And what course is the pirate on—can you tell—?"

Zinga came running toward them. "Pirate coming in on the same course—"

The officer turned and went inside the ship. Kartr drummed nervous fingers on the guard rail of the bridge. What in the name of Space was the fellow waiting for?

Then the sergeant was almost bowled over as five men flung themselves out of the hatchway and ran for the hall, taking both rangers with them. They had just reached the protection of the doorway when the Patrol ship took off.

Blinded by the sweep of flame Kartr clung to one of the pillars to keep his footing.

"What—?" he gasped.

And a babble of questions joined and drowned out his.

# 17

# THE END
# IS NOT YET

The hard surface of the partition ground into Kartr's back as the pressure of the crowd jammed him against that barrier. All the refugees were there in the narrow space behind the control table, tense, expectant, with no attention for anything but the sky map on the wall. Beside the sergeant a tall girl in the battle-stained tunic of a civilian supply assistant muttered half aloud to herself.

"There's only one of them—by the Grace of the Three—there is only one for him to face!"

Her "one" was that ominous red dot of the pirate ship still on course to Terra—headed without doubt for the very point on that planet where they now stood. But, even as they watched that advance helplessly, a second dot appeared on the screen—the Patrol ship moving out to meet the enemy.

"Time to try evasive!" Kartr caught the urgency in that man's voice rising from the mass of watchers. "Evade, Corris!"

And, as if that half-order half-plea had actually reached across space, the course of the Patrol ship changed. It seemed now as if it were attempting to make a futile run for safety, trying to elude the pirate. Out there a single brave man swung before a control panel, enmeshed in a pilot's web, prepared to fight a last battle to save his fellows. One lone Patrolman!

He continued to evade skillfully, altering his course just enough each time to draw the enemy after him, to persuade the other ship into pursuit and away from Terra. He had his screen up as the haze testified. That should act as a flaunting challenge to the pirate. The impulse of the pursuer would be to follow, to beat down the weak barrier, to put on a traction beam and warp in the Patrol ship. Only, what Captain Corris flew was no longer a ship, it was a single deadly weapon! And the enemy who strove to overtake and capture it would only trigger his own death in the same instant that he drew it in!

Kartr heard sobs, subdued, and little angry mutters from those about him.

"He has the tonite war head ready." That was the girl. She was talking as if to reassure herself, not to inform anyone else of what lay behind that silent battle out in the dark between worlds. "We were going to blow it if we were taken. He'll trigger it when they beam him in—" Her voice was hoarse, almost fierce.

The red dots moved as fighters sparring for an opening, making patterns on the screen. Kartr, though he was ignorant of space maneuvers, guessed that he was now watching the last fight of an inspired pilot. And yet to the pirate it must appear that a weak ship was trying desperately to escape.

"If only they don't suspect!" The girl's tone was that of a prayer. "Spirit of Space, keep them from suspecting—"

The end came as the Patrol pilot had planned it. A glow of battle screens hazed both ships—and then the one surrounding the Patrol ship disappeared. The dots moved toward each other—the pirate had clamped a pincher beam on its prey, was dragging the helpless ship to where

212

they could lock air-locks for boarding. At last the dots touched.

A flower of fire burst on the screen. It glowed for only a second and then died, to leave nothing behind it—nothing at all. The map was as blank as it had been when first they found it. Only the specks which were stars sparkled with aloof chill in the void.

No one in the crowd moved. It was as if they did not believe in the truth of what they had just witnessed, that they did not wish to believe. Then there was a single sigh and the tight mass broke apart. People drifted, with eyes which seemed to see nothing, out into the hall. Except for the shuffle of feet over the stone it was very quiet.

Overhead the gray light of another dawn gave a pale radiance. Kartr stepped up on the dais. He rested one hand on the back of the chair which was Terra's and looked closely for the first time at these new companions in misfortune.

They were a mixed lot, both as to race and species, as might be expected from a Patrol Ranger base. There were two more Zacathans, a pale-faced woman and two children with the goggles of the Faltharians hanging from their belts, and he was sure he had seen a feather crest which could only have graced the head of a Trystian.

"You are in command here?"

Kartr's attention flickered from the refugees to a girl—the same girl who had stood beside him to watch the battle—and two men standing together at the foot of the dais. Automatically Kartr's hand arose to touch a helmet he no longer wore.

"Ranger Sergeant Kartr of the Vegan *Starfire*. We crashed here some time ago. Our party consists of three other rangers, a com-techneer and an arms-techneer—"

"Medico-techneer Veelson," the shorter of the two men responded in a low and surprisingly musical voice. "This is Third Officer Moxan of our Base Ship, and Acting Ser-

213

geant Adrana of the Headquarters section. We are entirely at your service, Sergeant."

"Your party—"

"Our party," Veelson answered quickly, "numbers thirty-eight. Twenty women and six children are ranger dependents. Five crewmen under Moxan, and six supply corpswomen with Sergeant Adrana—and myself. As far as we know we are the only survivors of Base CC4."

"Zinga—Fylh—Rolth—" Kartr gave the order which came naturally to him. "Firewood detail and get some fires going—" He turned back to the medico-techneer. "I take it, sir, that you haven't much in the way of supplies?"

Veelson shrugged. "We have only what we could carry. It certainly isn't too much."

"A hunting party out, too, Zinga. Smitt, take over the communication board again. We don't want to be caught napping if there is another ship on its way. Any of your men know com, sir?" he asked Maxon.

Instead of answering directly the third officer turned on his heel and called down the length of the hall. "Havre!"

One of the men in crew uniform came running.

"Com work," his officer grunted. "Under this techneer."

"I take it that we can live off the country, since you mentioned hunting," Veelson asked.

"This is an Arth type planet. We've found it hospitable. In fact—this *is* Terra, you know."

Kartr watched the medico-techneer closely to see if that registered. It took a second or two, but it did.

"Terra." Veelson repeated the word blankly and then his eyes widened. "The home of the Lords of Space! But that is a legend—a fable!"

Kartr stamped on the dais. "Fairly substantial fable, don't you think? You are in the Hall of Leave-Taking now—look at the seats of the first star rangers, if you

214

wish." He pointed to the chairs. "Read what is carved on the back of this one. Yes, this is Terra of Sol!"

"Terra!" Veelson was still shaking his head wonderingly when Kartr spoke to the girl.

"You have your corpswomen. Can you take charge of the women and children?" he asked abruptly. This sort of duty was beyond his experience. He had established field camps, led expeditions, fought his way back and forth across many weird worlds in the past, but never before had he been responsible for such a group as this.

She started to nod, flushed, and raised her hand in salute. A moment later she was back circulating among the tired women and the fretful and too excited children—aided by the Zacathan family.

"Any chance of there being another pirate after you? What *did* happen at the base?" Already forgetting the women, Kartr began to question the medico-techneer.

"The base was wiped out. But things had begun to go wrong before that. There has been a breakdown somewhere along the supply and communication route. Our yearly supply ship was three months overdue even before the attack. We'd received no messages from Central Control for two weeks. We sent out a cruiser and it never returned.

"Then the pirate fleet came in. It was a *fleet* and the whole raid had been carefully planned. We had five ships on the field. Two raised and accounted for three of the pirates before they were blasted out. We manned the perimeter guns as long as we could and cleared the air for the survivors to take off.

"What caught us napping was that they came in under false colors and we accepted them as friendly until too late. They were Central Control ships! Either some section of the Fleet has mutinied or—or something terrible has happened to the whole empire. They acted as if the *Patrol* had been outlawed—their attack was vicious. And because they had come in with all the proper signals we weren't expecting it. It was as if *they* were the law—"

"Perhaps they are now," Kartr suggested grimly. "Maybe there has been a rebellion in this sector. The winner may be systematically mopping up all Patrol bases. That would leave him free to rule the space lanes as he pleases. A very practical and necessary move if there has been a change of government."

"That idea did occur to us. I can't say that we welcomed it." Veelson's voice was bleak. "Well, we did manage to crowd aboard a supply ship and one of the Patrol scouts. After that it was a running fight across space. They were between us and the regular routes so we had to head out this way. We lost the scout—"

Kartr nodded. "We saw that on the screen before we were able to contact you."

"It rammed a flagship—a flagship of the Fleet, mind you!"

"But effectively," the sergeant reminded him. "There were only the two ships following you—are you sure?"

"Only two registered on our screens. And—now if neither returns— Do you think that they will send another to track us down?"

"I don't know. They would accept the idea that the Patrol would be desperate enough to go out fighting. And so they may be willing to write off their ships as a case of blasting each other. But Smitt and your man can keep at their posts. They'll be able to give us warning in time if another heads this way."

"And if one does come?"

"Large portions of this world are wilderness. It will be easy to take to cover in plenty of time and they could never find us."

By the end of the day the new camp was well established. The hunting party had been successful enough so that everyone was fed. Under the leadership of the

216

corpswomen a party had spread out on the hill, hacked off branches, and fashioned beds. And there had been no warning—the screen in the hall remained blank.

It was night now. Kartr stood at the top of the stairs gazing down abstractedly at the landing field. A gleaning party had worked under his direction most of the afternoon, shifting the debris of the natives' encampment. And they had salvaged two spears and a handful of metal arrow points, treasures to be guarded against that day when the last blaster charge would be expended—when weapons which were the products of civilized skill would be useless.

Tomorrow they must hunt again and—

"A pleasant night, is it not, lady? There is, of course, only one moon instead of three. But it is a very bright one."

Kartr started and turned his head. Zicti was walking toward him accompanied by the girl, Adrana.

"Three moons? Is that the number which shine down on Zacan? Now I would consider two to be a more normal number." And she laughed.

Two moons. Kartr tried to remember all the two-mooned worlds he had known and wondered which had been her native one. But there were at least ten—and probably more which he had never heard of. No man, even if he had at least four lifetimes, could learn all that lay within the galaxy. Two moons was too faint a clue.

"Ha, the sergeant! So the night draws you also, my boy? One might believe that you were a Faltharian, this interest you show in a dark, sleeping world."

"Only doing some planning for the future," Kartr replied. "And I'm no Faltharian, only a barbarian," he added recklessly. "You know what they said of us of Ylene—that we eat raw meat and worship strange gods!"

"And you, lady," Zicti asked the girl, "upon which world did your two moons beam?"

She lifted her head with close to a defiant gesture, and stared out over the launching field as she answered.

"I was space born—a half-breed. My mother was of Krift. My father came from one of the outer system worlds, I don't know which. My two moon world I knew only for a short time when I was a small child. But I have seen many worlds for I am Service bred."

"We have all seen many worlds," Kartr observed, "and now I think we are going to learn one thoroughly."

Zicti inhaled the night air with gusto. "But such a pleasant world, my children. I must say that I have great hopes for our future here."

"It is good to know that someone has," Kartr said somberly.

But it was Adrana who rose to the Zacathan's challenge. "You are right!" She laid her fingers on the hist-techneer's scaled arm. "This *is* a good world! When I was up on the hill today, the air was like wine in my throat. It is free—alive! And we are very lucky. For the first time in my life"—she paused as if she were surprised at her own words—"I feel at home!"

"Because this is Terra—racial memory—" suggested Kartr.

"I don't know. After so long a time—that couldn't be possible, could it?"

"Perhaps." He added a confession of his own. "The first day we landed here—when I saw the green of this vegetation—it seemed then that I, too, remembered."

"Well, children, I do *not* remember Terra, nor can any of my race. But still I say that we have landed on a good world—a pleasant one to make our own. We have only to do that—"

"What of the city and the clans?" inquired the sergeant. "Are they going to sit passive and allow us such usurpation?"

"This is a wide world. And that problem we shall face

218

when it arises. Now, moon gazers, not being a Faltharian, I shall seek my bedroll. You must pardon my withdrawal." Chuckling he padded away.

"What did you mean—the city and the clans? Are there natives here?" questioned the girl.

"Yes." Briefly Kartr gave her the facts. "So you see," he ended, "this world is not altogether ours for the taking. And since we cannot remain at this point on it indefinitely we shall have decisions to make soon."

She nodded. "Tell the others tomorrow. Tell them all you have told me."

"You mean—leave the decision up to them? All right." He shrugged.

What if they chose the comfort of the city? Such a decision would only be natural. But, he was very sure, he would not go back there nor would the others who had followed him out of that monument to a too-ancient past.

Because he agreed that each must decide for him- or herself, he stood again the next morning in the pool of hot sunlight which crossed the dais. His throat was dry. He had been talking steadily. And now he was tired, as tired as if he had spent half the day cutting through heavy brush. Those faces all turned to him, so impassive, so controlled.

Had any of them really heard what he had been saying, or having heard, did they understand? Was this indifference the result of their immediate past, were they sure that the worst had already happened and that nothing could shake them again?

"And that is the situation we now face—"

But there was no response from the seated refugees. Then he heard the scrape of bootsoles across the pavement, sounding louder because of the silence in the hall. Veelson jumped up on the dais to join him.

"We have the report of the ranger sergeant. He gives

219

us two courses which may be followed. First—we may try to contact this civilian party now occupying a city not too far distant, a city with part of its functions restored. But they have the problem of limited food supply and in addition"—the medico-techneer paused, and then he added without any change of tone or expression—"that party is an entirely human one."

Again there was no response from the listeners. Had they met with anti-Bemmy feeling before? They must have! It had been growing so powerful. But if they had it made no difference. In the wide seat marked Deneb was the Faltharian woman and she cradled in her arms a tiny Trystian whose mother had not survived the base raid. And Zor sat between two inner system boys of his own age. There was no drawing apart in this company— Bemmy to Bemmy, human to human. These were the rangers!

"So we may go to the city," Veelson repeated, "or we may choose the second solution which could mean a much greater measure of hardship. Though we of the rangers, by training and tradition, are better able to face what it may demand of us. And that is to live on the land after the fashion of the natives.

"Sergeant Kartr has spoken of a cold season reported to be approaching now. He has also pointed out that we cannot remain here—due to lack of supplies. We can travel south—as the majority of the natives did when they left here a few days ago. Contact with the natives, while impossible now—judging by the sergeant's unfortunate experience—may be allowed later as we have some medical supplies and knowledge. But it might be years before we dare attempt such fraternization.

"These are the two choices we are now assembled to vote upon—"

"Medico Veelson!" One of the crewmen was on his

feet. "Do you rule out all possibility of rescue then? Couldn't we remain near here and try to use that communicator to summon help? Any Patrol ship—"

"Any *Patrol* ship!" Again the lack of expression in the medico-techneer's voice underlined his words. "A communication attempt might just as well bring down roving pirates upon us. There is no way of identifying until too late any ship we might be able to beam in. And remember, Terra is off every known chart—so forgotten that its name is now only a legend."

A murmur ran from seat to seat.

"So we must accept exile?" That was a woman.

"I believe that we must." Veelson's answer came clear and firm.

Another silence followed. They were facing the truth now. And—Kartr thought proudly—they were accepting it quietly.

"I believe that we wish to remain together—" Veelson continued slowly.

"Yes!" That answer was so loud it woke a faint echo from the roof. The Patrol would stand together, that creed which had been theirs for generations still held them.

"We will abide by the will of the majority. Those who wish to seek shelter in the city may take their places against that wall. Those who would remain apart—on the land—stand here—"

Veelson had not even finished speaking before he himself moved with two distance-eating strides to the left of the dais. And Kartr joined him. Only for a moment were they alone. Adrana and her six co-workers arose from their seats in the group and marched to stand beside the medico-techneer. But then there was a pause—the other women did not move.

It was the Faltharian woman who broke the spell. Still

carrying the Trystian infant and pushing her own two children ahead, she walked quickly to the left. But she did not reach the others before Zicti and his family.

Now there was a steady shuffling of feet and when it was quiet again there was no need to count heads. Not one stood on the city side. They had made their decision, weighing the evidence and the chances of the future. And, Kartr knew, seeing their serene faces, they would stand by it. Suddenly he was vaguely sorry for those in the city. They would struggle there to keep up a measure of mechanical civilization. Perhaps they would live in greater ease for this generation. But in a way they had turned their backs upon the future and they might not be allowed a second choice.

But the Patrol were eager to be gone, once their minds were made up. And the dawn of the second day saw them in marching order, their scanty belongings in packs, their faces set toward the unknown lands of the south.

Kartr watched Fylh and Zinga lead that line of women and children, crewmen and officers, all one now under an alien sun, going into the future.

He glanced back into the deserted hall. The sun caught and held on the symbols in the captains' seats along one side. Old Terra— And down there—heading into the wilderness was the NEW!

"Shall we rise again to be the lords of space and the rangers of the star lanes?" he wondered. "Do we begin this day a second cycle leading to another empire?"

He was a little startled when Zicti's thought answered his. "It is just history, my boy, history. We fashion that whether or no. But there is a very old saying known to my people—'When a man comes to the end of any road let him remember that the end is not yet and a new way shall open for him.' "

Kartr turned his back upon the Hall of Leave-Taking

222

and ran lightly down the eroded steps. The wind was chill but the sun was warm. Dust puffed up from beneath the marching feet.

"Yes, the end is not yet! Let us go!"